Crazy Grandma Genius Baby

and me!

H.J. Hewett

CHAPTER 1

People sometimes wonder about Einstein's mother. What was she like? What did she do that made Einstein turn out to be a genius? But it's the grandmothers you have to watch out for. No one tells you about Einstein's grandmother.

My grandma is crazy and my four-year-old kid brother Toby is a genius. My mom is a food scientist. My dad is also super smart and has a degree in Engineering. We get mail at our house addressed to Dr. and Dr. Westly.

Then there's me, Theo, non-genius. I spend most of my time hanging out with my best friend Darnell and trying to keep Grandma and Toby out of trouble. It's a full-time job. Yesterday they nearly burned the house down.

I'm sure it all started innocently. Toby probably asked something like, "Grandma, do things that are heavier go up in the air slower?" and Grandma said, "Let's find out!"

Normal people might have constructed a catapult, the kind you can make at home with rubber bands and a plastic spoon, but we're talking about Grandma and Toby.

They began by modifying my arrow rocket launcher. Then one of them, I never found out which, suggested using chemical rather than kinetic energy, and they moved on to constructing a potato cannon. The REAL trouble started when Grandma dragged out the air compressor tank from the garage and they started experimenting with butane and rubbing alcohol. My grandma is seriously insane! I don't know why Mom and Dad think she and my brother can be left alone together.

One of their homemade rockets spun out of control and whizzed around the house until it made a hole in the dining room wall. Another exploded and started a small fire. It was a good thing I got home when I did because Grandma and Toby were in the middle of a discussion about how much force it would take to achieve escape velocity from Earth. Plus I was in time to help them put out the fire they had forgotten was still burning. It took longer than usual because first we had to FIND the fire extinguisher, which, it turned out, had been rigged to Toby's tricycle. Neither Grandma nor Toby would admit having done it, which means they were probably both in on it together.

The answer to Toby's original question, by the way, is yes. If you were curious. Lighter objects do go up in the air faster, but everything comes down at the same speed ($9.81m/s^2$), which is kind of weird if you think about it.

I probably should have been paying more attention in Science class, because then Mr. Henley said, "And that'll be on Thursday's test."

Wait, what? There's a test on Thursday? Since when? And what was it that he just said was going to be on it? But Mr. Henley was already wiping off the whiteboard with his big eraser. Mr. Henley LOVES physics. I mean, he gets excited about levers and pulleys and stuff like that. My brother Toby only gets really excited about things that are gross or explode, preferably both. I started wondering what else was going to be on the test. Maybe Darnell would help me study for it.

I wished I could ask Katrina to study with me. I suppose every guy thinks the girl he has a crush on is the prettiest girl in the school, and Katrina is the smartest, sweetest, prettiest girl I've ever known. I couldn't help sneaking a look at her over my shoulder, but then I saw our school bully, Stewart Potts, giving me the stink-eye, so I quickly looked back at the whiteboard.

Mr. Henley was writing on it and saying, "And don't forget—" He backed up and there in block letters were the words "All-School FunFest Thursday." I groaned out loud. "FunFest" at our school meant a Bake-Off contest. Did I mention my mom is a food scientist?? Mr. Henley kept talking as he passed out bright orange handouts with the FunFest information. I stuffed the flier down as far as I could into the bottom of my backpack. I didn't hear a word. This was a catastrophe. I'd have to come up with a plan.

CHAPTER 2

After school Darnell and I met up at the ABB. It's a good place to hang out because it's a block from school. We all call it the ABB, but it's actually "Arlo's Burgers and Brats." Arlo is Darnell's dad. I like Arlo because he always gives me free food.

Nobody else knows it, but Darnell and I look out after each other, food-wise. Every morning Darnell's dad makes him an amazing hoagie sandwich and then Stew-Pot steals it on our way to school. So I split my lunch money with Darnell and he asks his dad make us something to eat after school before I go home for dinner. Arlo doesn't know. He just gives me burgers or whatever because I'm Darnell's friend.

It's a good arrangement, because dinner at my house can be *interesting,* like the time my mom was experimenting with cucumber noodles and strawberry jam spaghetti sauce.

"So there's going to be a Science test Thursday?" I asked Darnell.

His dad came out of the back kitchen, rubbing his hands on his striped apron. "How're my favorite customers?"

"Fine," Darnell mumbled.

"What can I get you boys?" he asked.

"I'd like two hot dogs," I piped up.

"Yeah, that sounds okay," Darnell said.

"Coming right up!" Darnell's dad said, ringing his own counter bell. "How was school today, son?" he asked.

"Fine, Dad."

"Yeah, okay," his dad said, laughing. "You two go grab your table."

When we sat down, Darnell reached into his backpack and silently pushed something across the table to me. It was one of those "Wish You Were Here" postcards from the Virgin Islands. Darnell's mom is a flight attendant.

"Oh," I said and pushed it back to him. I tried to cheer him up. "Hey, want to come back to my house after school? I still have three lunar modules to build to make the Space Mech Mega Robot."

"Cool!" Darnell agreed.

Darnell's dad came over with the hot dogs loaded up with ketchup, mustard, peppers, pickles, and onions, the way I like them.

"Awesome! Thanks, Mr. Samuels." I started shoveling food in my mouth. We had only had half a lunch each, and we were pretty hungry.

"What are you going to do about the FunFest?" Darnell asked.

"What do you mean, what am I going to do about it?" I asked, playing dumb.

"Dude!" Darnell said. "Your mom!"

"Oh that," I said lamely.

"Isn't she going to want to bring something??"

"Maybe I can tell her there won't be a Bake-Off this year."

Darnell looked doubtful. "I don't know. Your mom's pretty smart, Theo."

"Don't worry so much," I said. "I'm on it. I'll think of something."

"Yeah, you'd better," Darnell said, "because

you don't want her showing up with something weird like those pepperoni biscuits. It took me two days to get the taste out of my mouth. Man, even Einstein wouldn't touch them."

Einstein is our family dog, a German shepherd mutt, who must be smarter than I am, because he took one sniff and backed away.

"They were pretty salty," I admitted. "Mom means well. She just gets bored making regular food and she likes being creative. Which could be cool . . . "

"If somebody didn't have to eat it," Darnell finished. He had already eaten both of his hot dogs and I saw I'd better hurry up. For a skinny kid, he can make a serious dent in a basket of French fries. All of a sudden, though, Darnell froze and got really quiet, so I knew something was up.

"Don't look," Darnell hissed at me, which is

one of the dumber things you can say to a person, because then the person can't HELP but look.

I was fairly sure what I was going to see, but I turned around anyway, and there she was.

I may have mentioned Katrina is super cute. She has long brown hair in a braid, eyes that sparkle, and a smile so sweet it knocks you over flat. She's really friendly too, and always cheerful, and she has a normal family with a real stay-at-home mom who cuts the crusts off the Wonder Bread sandwiches in Katrina's lunch. I don't remember my mom EVER doing that for me, even when I was little.

I don't mind that Darnell likes Katrina too, because, let's face it, *all* the guys in our middle school have had a crush on her since she moved here. I ate the rest of my hot dog while we watched her laughing with her friends on the track team. Darnell sits next to her in Science class, but we both knew that was probably the closest either of us would get to Katrina Bixby. If middle school was a biome, we lived in what Mr. Henley would call separate ecosystems.

When we were done eating, I wadded up the wrappers and dumped everything into the trash bin to get rid of the evidence. I'd hate to have to explain to Mom why I'd been eating fast-food before dinner.

"Ready to walk home, D?" I heaved my backpack onto my shoulder.

"Yeah, okay," Darnell agreed.

"I'd better see what Grandma and Genius Baby are up to."

"Make sure the house is still standing," Darnell added.

CHAPTER 3

At first I thought Grandma and Toby had set the house on fire again, because thick white smoke was billowing up out of our yard and settling over the neighbors' houses.

"Let 'er rip!" we heard Grandma shout as Darnell and I came running up to the back gate. There was another huge cloud of smoke.

We started coughing and waving our hands. When the smoke cleared, there were Grandma and Toby, wearing face masks, standing over my mom's chemistry ring stand and something that looked like a tiny space capsule made out of the dome of a plastic soda bottle taped to a pie plate.

Grandma took off her face mask and said, "Oh hello, Darnell," very politely. "Won't you join us?" Sure, she looks harmless in her flower-print dresses and wool cardigans. Her fluffy white hair is in a bun, and she has these cute round pink cheeks and a tiny chin with a little puckered up mouth and crinkly blue eyes, but as I've told Darnell before, you can't let that fool you.

"How does it work?" Darnell asked.

"D!" I objected. Asking just encourages Grandma. I love her and all, but the woman is a menace. I never got to know my grandpa. He died before I was born. He was an engineer, and deaf in one ear. I bet that was because of one of Grandma's experiments. Mom says he was very kind, gentle, and soft-spoken, but then Mom thinks Grandma is an innocent old lady who wouldn't hurt a fly, so there's really no telling.

"Well, now," said Grandma, "Toby was just asking me this morning about condensation and evaporation. So we took a soda bottle from the Nesbitts' recycling bin, cut off the top, and taped it onto this pie plate. You put the whole thing over a heat source, like a candle underneath."

"Or an acetylene torch," my kid brother Toby added helpfully.

Grandma frowned at him, which meant the acetylene torch was supposed to be secret. "The candle heats up the pie plate," she explained, bending over to show Darnell the set up. "Then you add a drop or two of homemade fog juice."

"Fog juice?" Darnell asked, interested.

Grandma held out the bottle to show him. "When it's heated, the glycerin and water evaporate and turn into gas." She coughed and waved away a cloud of smoke. "I may have added a little too much."

"Cool!" Darnell agreed.

"I'm pretty sure it's safe," Grandma added. She winked at us.

Darnell took a quick step backwards, just in case.

"Where's Einstein?" I asked.

"Not to worry," Toby said, "you put a face mask on him too."

Toby always says 'you' when he means 'I' and 'I' when he means 'you.' My four-year-old brother can do my fifth grade Math and Science AND Spanish homework in his head, but

English he gets wrong every time. Mom says Toby is going through a linguistic phase, evolving his own grammar from the raw building blocks of our language. She says it has something to do with his brain moving faster than he can talk, which is alarming, because Toby talks pretty fast, if you ask me. Mom says we shouldn't pressure his development by correcting him, so I let what he said about Einstein go. Besides, there were more pressing topics of conversation.

"Why is there a propane tank on our lawn?" I asked.

Grandma side-stepped in front of it. "What propane tank?"

Toby piped up. "We tried that first. But it turns out mineral oil is a highly flammable substance," he added. Then he saw Grandma's warning look and stopped talking. Apparently the mineral oil was supposed to be a secret too.

Einstein poked his head through the pet door he uses to come and go out of the kitchen at the back of the house. He trotted down the steps to join us. He was indeed wearing a face mask, with the elastic hooked over his big ears. I took it off of him and he licked my hands, just in case there was anything tasty left over.

"Come on," I said. "Let's go get the fans before the Nesbitts call the fire department again."

"Cripes! Did I forget to close the windows?" Grandma exclaimed in surprise.

Mr. and Mrs. Nesbitt live in the house to our left. They are nice people, but they tend to worry too much. We dragged out every fan in the house, including one stuck up in the attic, and set them all on high. The noise was like being inside a jet engine.

When we turned off the fans, we heard someone ringing the doorbell and knocking loudly at the front door.

CHAPTER 4

Just a minute!" Grandma called and went shuffling down the hall to answer the door.

"Oh Mrs. Nesbitt, how are you?" we heard my grandma say. "Oh no, dear. We're all fine. No need to call 911. How very neighborly of you to ask. So thoughtful. Good-bye!"

Grandma came back into the living room as if nothing strange had happened. She sat down in her favorite spot on the sofa and picked up her latest latch hook. She doesn't knit, or do crochet like normal grandmas. She does latch hook rugs and hangings, with awful things like cuddly kittens with pink bows and horses racing past sunsets. Whenever Grandma finishes one, Mom feels she has to do something with it, so Grandma's latch hooks are framed and hung up all over the house. They come in handy sometimes when you have to cover something up. Like scorch marks or the hole left by a runaway rocket.

I turned to Toby. "You better put Mom's chemistry ring stand back where it belongs," I told him sternly.

"You didn't damage it," Toby said, sulking.

"I'm still pretty sure Mom doesn't want you playing with her stuff," I said.

Toby suddenly smiled and asked Darnell, "Do I want to hold some snot?" He had a sly look as he put his hand into his pants pocket.

"What?" Darnell asked, but it was too late. Toby pulled out a plastic bag and dumped something yellow and green and slimy into Darnell's hand.

"YUCK!" Darnell said, mushing it around with his finger and making it stretch. "What is it?"

"Mostly glue and water, also food coloring," said Toby. He LOVES talking about his weird little science projects to anyone who will listen.

"And an eighth-cup borax," I said, "which is a dangerous chemical. You know Mom doesn't want you messing with that stuff by yourself."

"Grandma helped you," Toby said defensively.

"Uh, I'm going to go wash my hands now," Darnell said.

"Go away," I said to Toby. "Come on, I

mean it, get lost. D and I have things to do."

"What things?"

"Secret things. Shoo."

When I was four, I really, REALLY wanted a kid brother. I thought it would be so much fun to have someone who would play with me. My parents bought a dog instead, which my dad named "Einstein," after his hero, because no one in my family can do something normal.

Then a couple years later Toby came along. I thought it was sort of neat at first, but he turned out to be creepy smart and even weirder than my parents, and now he follows me around everywhere and wants to know everything I'm doing. It's SO annoying.

"The last time I let you play with my solar-powered robot kit, you patched it into Einstein's collar and reconfigured the radio control to emit a 44 kilohertz pitch whenever he drank from the toilet bowl, so No, go away," I said.

Toby's face collapsed in an unhappy frown. "It was part of an aversion therapy study," he said.

"Don't you know positive reinforcement training methods are generally held to be more effective?" I scolded him.

Toby's frown got deeper. "Mom and Dad would have been happy if it had worked," he said.

"You're just lucky Mom and Dad *don't* know," I pointed out. "Dad would never have bought you that soldering kit if he had known what you were going to use it for."

Einstein just looked at us with his big, sad-looking eyes and panted with his tongue hanging out. He LOVES Toby.

CHAPTER 5

"Theo?" Mom said as she set out the dinner plates in front of us. She hadn't told us yet what dinner was, so I poked at it with a fork. Eggplant was definitely involved. And maybe some kind of egg custard. Or maybe a mustardy-mayonnaise. It could easily be banana pudding, knowing my mom.

Dad was happily digging in. He either has no taste buds, or he really loves my mom and doesn't want to hurt her feelings, possibly both. Grandma just takes dainty little bites, and Toby was using his fingers to search for bits that might be edible, but nobody minds because he's four and kids his age are supposed to be picky. Personally, I suspect he and Grandma have some other secret source of nutrients to keep them going like I do. Maybe they invented their own super food cubes in my mom's downstairs lab. Yes, my mom has a lab in our basement. Seriously, how weird is that?

"Theo?" Mom said again, because I hadn't been paying attention.

"Yeah, Mom?"

"You didn't tell me about the school FunFest on Thursday." Her tone was gentle with just a hint of sad surprise.

"I forgot," I mumbled.

"I found the flier all crumpled up in your

school backpack today—"

"Mom! You went through my backpack? You're not supposed to touch my stuff!"

"Honey!" she said. "I just needed to take out your gym socks to put in the laundry. You left them all bunched up inside your backpack and it was driving Einstein crazy."

I gave him a dirty look under the table. He whined and put his head between his paws, waiting for something to drop off of Toby's plate. Did you know dogs can eat things like green beans and carrots and even pumpkin?

"I just wish you'd ask me first," I muttered and used my fork to move the food around on my plate to make it look like I had been eating.

"What's in this, Zee?" my father asked. "This is delicious!" *Zee* is the nickname my dad uses for my mom. Her real name is Zenobia, and that alone should tell you my grandma is not all right in the head.

But Mom was off and running. "I think I could take off early Thursday from the lab." The research lab where she works, not the lab in our basement. "I wonder if I could make a sort of blueberry shortcake bar," she went on dreamily, "but with sausage instead of crumble on top."

I shot a glance over at Grandma, but she was eating tiny forkfuls and looking perfectly innocent.

I was instantly suspicious. I looked over at Toby, but he was making a face at something stringy he had picked off his plate. He even eats things that you wouldn't think could be eaten with your fingers, like cottage cheese. By the end of dinner, everything is always mixed together and he's smeared with food up to his elbows. He's so gross.

Toby saw me looking at him and he leaned over in his chair to whisper, "Did I know that in Thailand people eat *ant larvae??*"

Like I said, EEEW!

I went back to watching Grandma across the table, trying to guess what the two of them were planning. When she gets that sweet-old-lady-minding-my-own-business-look, watch out!

I cleared my throat, still keeping an eye on Grandma. "Um, what about one of those store-bought mixes, Mom? Or, you know, something from the bakery? I mean, then you wouldn't even have to cook, right?"

I knew I had said the wrong thing because Mom dropped her fork. "Theodore!" she exclaimed, making sure I grasped the enormity of the situation by using my full name, which is kept on reserve for just such occasions. "Do you know what's IN those things? Yellow dye

Number 5, propylene glycol diester, monocalcium phosphate—"

I stopped listening and went back to toying with the food on my plate. So much for that strategy. I would have to come up with something better.

"Has that latch hook with the kittens always been here in the dining room?" Dad asked. "I thought it used to be in the upstairs hallway."

CHAPTER 6

Darnell was waiting for me like usual on the front steps the next morning. We cut across the backyard and through the alley to the next street. After we turned the corner and were out of sight, Darnell dug in his backpack and handed me a breakfast burrito. It was kind of cold by now, but it still tasted better than the mocha mushroom pancakes Mom made for breakfast.

"Did your mom say what she's bringing to the FunFest Thursday?" Darnell asked.

"I told you, I'm gonna take care of it. I just haven't figured out how yet."

"At least you mom's around to bring something to the FunFest," Darnell said. "My mom texted me she's in Costa Rica. My dad'll probably bring something, though. He makes those really good chocolate éclair things. Hey," Darnell suggested, "why don't you ask your dad if he'd bring something this year?"

I frowned. "I'm not sure if my dad can cook. He's good with bridges and skyscrapers and things, but I've only ever seen him use the microwave."

Darnell shook his head. "You better hope he comes through for you, Theo. You remember that year your mom made the inside-out Thanksgiving turkey?" He shivered. "If you can't think of something in time to stop your mom . . . I wouldn't want to be in your shoes."

"I know, I know. I'll handle it. Quit worrying. What kind of sandwich did your dad make for you?" I asked to change the subject.

"Pastrami Reuben, why?"

"I just wondered what Stew-Pot would be eating today. Hey, do you think after school we could go over to your house and play with your quad-copter?"

"Sure," Darnell agreed. "You can even fly it a little, if you want. We can take turns."

He really is a good friend.

I used to have a remote-control alien orb, but the manufacturers who claimed it was "virtually indestructible" had clearly never met Toby the Genius Baby.

"Count Dooku and the Mandalorians on interception course," I said. We've tried to avoid Stew-Pot by coming around the K-4 buildings, but eventually you have to cross the small parking lot to get to the 5-8 entrance, and he's always waiting there with his buddies.

"Yeah," said Darnell. We both took a tighter hold on the straps of our backpacks.

Stew-Pot is one of those tough, wiry kids—small, but really mean. He always wears this red baseball cap backwards on his head. He thinks it makes him look tougher. He's right. It does.

He also employs a group of ape-like mammals who do his bidding. They closed ranks and surrounded us. No escape.

"Check his pockets, Mikey," Stew-Pot ordered.

CHAPTER 7

I'm telling you I don't have any lunch money on me," I lied.

Mike Vickers, a.k.a. Mikey the Hammer, lumbered over. They're like the middle school version of super soldiers. I'm pretty sure test tubes were involved somewhere, because no normal human beings were meant to be this large at our age.

We went through the ritual of turning out my

pockets. First the jacket, then the pants. I insist on turning out my own pants pockets to show they're empty. A man has his pride.

"How's the weather up in the jet stream?" I asked Mikey. Float like a butterfly, sting like a bee.

No response.

I tried another one. "Hey Mikey, does your mom have to buy your clothes somewhere special, or does the kid's section have a Big & Tall?"

"Shut up, Westly," Stew-Pot said.

Actually, when it comes to combat, my main strategies are 1. Hide like a chameleon, and 2. Run like a rabbit. My backup strategies are 3. Playing dead like an opossum, and 4. Slinking away like a weasel.

"Nothing in his pockets, boss," Mikey reported.

"Thank you, Captain Obvious," I said, pulling myself back together. "I told you I didn't have anything on me."

Having failed yet again to figure out where I keep my lunch money, Stew-Pot moved on to the main event.

"Hand over the sandwich, creep," he said to Darnell.

Darnell held it out.

Mikey took the bag over to Stew-Pot.

Stew-Pot slid the sandwich out and began to unwrap it slowly. This was also part of the ritual.

I will say for Stew-Pot that he unwrapped that sandwich like the thing of wonder it was. Two, thick, toasty slices of marbled rye, piled high with shaved pastrami, melted Swiss cheese, dressing, and tangy sauerkraut.

Stew-Pot took a big bite and stood there,

chewing. He was making me hungry, the way he was enjoying that sandwich.

"I'm going to save the rest of this for later. Mmm-mm," he said, licking Thousand Island from his lips and patting his stomach, "these sandwiches your dad makes sure are DEE-licious. A lot better than anything you can get at the cafeteria, boy."

"Okay, okay," I said, pretending like I was bored. "You got your sandwich. Can we go now? I don't want to be late to school."

He snorted.

"Mr. Jennings is really strict about Homeroom. I don't want to get marked late," I said. People experience fear in different ways. Darnell clams up. I turn into a motor-mouth.

"Yeah, whatever. Get lost," Stew-Pot said. He jerked his head at Team Thug and they lumbered off like a herd of meat-eating dinosaurs in search of their next snack.

Darnell had just been silent the entire time. He looked miserable like usual, but what are you going to do? It doesn't pay to mess with jerks like Stew-Pot.

Darnell and I split a personal-size pizza for lunch. Sometimes we get the chicken nuggets, or mac-and-cheese, or the nacho-taco salad, but pizza is our favorite. I felt bad because it was my day to have the milk, so I let Darnell eat most of the corn chips, although that might not have been such a good idea because he had to get up a lot to go to the water fountain.

Darnell said, "If my Lego Corsair Pirate ship was in a fight with your Black Pearl, which one do you think would win?"

"Are Aragorn, Legolas, and Gimli fighting Jack Sparrow, Will, and Gibbs, or are they joining forces to fight the Orcs and Davy Jones?"

"Ship against ship," Darnell said.

I had to think about it. "Well, it's nine against six, counting the Pirate of Umbar. That doesn't seem like really fair odds."

Darnell wasn't impressed. "You have pistols as well as swords. The only range weapons my guys have are a crossbow and Legolas' longbow."

"What about the Orc catapult?" I asked.

"Against the Pearl's starboard cannons?" Darnell pointed out. It was a good point.

"Yeah, but you've still got more guys. Plus, if you came at me head on, you could use the ram."

"Maybe this Saturday I could bring the Corsair over and we could see who wins."

"We'd better do it at your house," I said,

taking a drink of milk. "We don't want Genius Baby getting into our stuff."

I ate for a moment in silence while I thought about Saturday's fight some more. Then I shook my head. "I just really don't think Jack would get into a fight with Aragorn. He's much too cool for that."

Suddenly, mid-bite, Darnell froze.

CHAPTER 8

Katrina Bixby came over to our table. I mean actually walked over and talked to us. Even I went numb, like a small fish stung by the tentacles of a Portuguese man o' war. People confuse the Portuguese man o' war with jellyfish, but they're siphonophores, which means a Portuguese man o' war is actually a colony of these individual tentacle-animals called zooids working together, like my six-in-one Space Mech Mega Robot. How weird is that? My dad told me about zooids once.

"Oh hey, Darnell!" Then Katrina turned her sunshine smile on me. "And you're Darnell's friend."

"Theo," I said. I considered holding out my hand like I've seen my dad or mom do, but then I thought she might think that was strange, so I didn't.

"Oh yeah. You're in Mr. Henley's Science class too, aren't you?"

"Yeah," I said, real casual-like, but my heart was beating fast. This was IT! My moment to make a good impression.

"Maybe we could all get together Wednesday night to study for the test," she suggested. "What do you think? We could get together at the library, or someone's house."

"Not mine," I put in quickly. "Not that

there's anything wrong with my house. I mean, my house is fine, but I don't think my parents would like it. Us studying. Ha ha! Of course, they want us to study. It's a big test, isn't it? Just not there." Katrina was giving me a funny look. I was talking way too fast. "The library sounds great!" I finished, lamely with a big smile.

"What about meeting up at the ABB?" she suggested.

"My dad is the owner," Darnell said, suddenly finding his voice.

"Wow, really? Your dad is Arlo?" Katrina asked. "He makes the best chili-cheese dogs ever!"

"You like chili-cheese dogs?" Darnell asked.

"Are you kidding me? With raw onions on top? Who doesn't?" Katrina said. She laughed, but I think she was being serious.

I made a face at Darnell over her shoulder, but he wasn't looking at me. Just basking in the radiance that is Katrina Bixby.

"Yeah, I like them too," Darnell said, which was a lie, and he knew I knew it was a lie, and I was totally sitting right there but he said it anyway.

Stew-Pot crossed the far end of the cafeteria and pointed at our table in a way that said, *I've got my eye on you two.* Darnell and I did our best to blend into the orange plastic chairs.

"Is Stewart mean to you?" Katrina asked.

"You could say that," I said.

"You know, most bullies have been really hurt themselves."

"Tragic," I said.

My phone dinged. I checked it. A text from Toby: *Where does mom keep the anhydrous magnesium sulfate?*

CHAPTER 9

I don't know who in my family taught Toby how to use a smartphone. Being Toby, he probably held it to his forehead and downloaded the user manual straight into his giant brain. Anyway, Mom bought him his own phone, "in case of emergencies," she said. Hilarious. Toby doesn't have emergencies. Toby causes emergencies. Besides, I'm convinced he's one of those creatures with nine lives that never gets hurt. That's the only explanation for why both he and Grandma still have ten fingers and toes. At least I think they do. I haven't checked their feet recently.

I texted back: *WHY* and then immediately followed it with: *Never mind just stop whatever it is you're doing STOP.*

"Are you okay, Theo?" Katrina was looking at me funny again.

"Huh? Yeah. Of course." I tried to laugh. It came out sounding strange.

"You have to stand up to bullies," Katrina said earnestly.

"Um, yeah, back here on planet *Earth,*" I said. Even a non-genius like me could tell you standing up to a bully like Stew-Pot just means leaving a Theo Westly-shaped smear in the asphalt.

My phone dinged again.

Grandma found it.

"Oh no, no, no!" I said. I still had four periods left before I could get home to inspect the wreckage. Maybe I could get out early if I told Mrs. Delgado fifth period there'd been a sudden death in the family. It was possible.

"If people let bullies get away with whatever they want, they just keep taking advantage of others," Katrina was saying. She's one of those people who are so sweet and sincere, like my mom, that you can't stay annoyed at them for long.

"Yep, that's what happens," I agreed. "Don't you remember Mr. Henley talking about food webs? Some of us have to be plankton. Circle of life. Come on, D," I said, standing up.

The bell rang.

"Bye, Darnell," Katrina said.

We shouldered our backpacks. Darnell had a

dopey smile on his face.

Okay, so that could have gone a lot better, I thought as I walked to class. I didn't exactly get off on the right foot with Katrina, but I'm pretty sure a spark was there. I think we made a connection. At least now she knows my name, right?

I woke up early the next morning with a bad feeling I couldn't explain in the pit of my stomach. I got dressed and went downstairs where I found Toby, still in his Spider-Man pajamas, raiding the fruit and vegetable bin in the glow of the open refrigerator. He had his arms full of cabbage and apples and pears. He looked around when I flicked on the overhead light.

"What are you doing?" I asked.

"Do I know where you can get *Tenebrio*

molitor larvae?" he asked.

I started to say, "I don't know, *do* you know," like I usually do and then my brain caught up.

"Mealworms," Toby explained, when I didn't answer right away because my mouth was hanging open. "Preferably in bulk."

"Ick! No! And put those back, before Mom finds out."

"They make the best subjects for biological research!" Toby protested. "The book from the library says they are easy to rear and handle."

"I said, no! Double-ick. Come on, get back to bed. You're not supposed to be up yet." I pushed the refrigerator bin shut and closed the door.

"Did I know each female lays about 500 eggs at a time?" Toby said happily.

"That's really disgusting," I said. "And I

better not catch you in the fridge again."

Toby gave me his sad, hurt look and padded off.

And that was just the start of my horrible day.

Darnell only shook his head when I told him about it on our walk to school.

"Man, your family is *weird*," he agreed. Nothing I tell him surprises him anymore.

I sighed. "I had no idea how hard it was going to be having a kid brother around," I said. "My parents are lucky I'm there to look after him. What's Stew-Pot have for lunch today?"

"My dad made a Black Forest ham and Swiss sandwich, with honey mustard," Darnell said. There was something strange about the way he said it. Something un-Darnell.

"Sounds good," I said. "Hey, it's your turn

for the milk box at lunch today. You want chocolate or regular?"

"I dunno," Darnell said.

"You want to split mac-and-cheese or pizza today?"

"Maybe let's not talk about food right now," Darnell said. We were getting close to the lot where Stew-Pot and his gorilla gang like to hang out.

"Yeah, okay," I said. I curled my toe around the lunch money in my shoe and took a better grip on my backpack. I hated this part of the morning and just wanted to get it over with.

"How's it going, Mikey?" I asked as we turned out my pockets. This kid's hands are so big he has to use his thumb and one finger.

"Okay, I guess," said Mikey.

"This is good!" I said. "Now you say, 'How's it going, Theo?' In a friendly way. Like you care."

"Uh, how's it going, Theo?" Mikey said.

Stew-Pot interrupted. "Shut up, Westly," he said. "And you too, idiot," he said to Mikey. "Go get my sandwich."

Mikey hung his head. "Sorry, Stew."

"It's okay, big guy," I said to his retreating back. "I felt like we made progress today. We were dialoguing. Starting to have a conversation."

Darnell had a really funny look on his face when Mikey put out his hand. I should have known then that something bad was going to happen.

CHAPTER 10

For a minute nothing happened at all.

I nudged Darnell. Honestly, it was embarrassing, like being on stage with a kid who's forgotten his lines. "Give him the sandwich, D," I said in a low voice.

But Darnell had not forgotten. Darnell was having none of it today. He rushed past Mikey like a little dark tornado cloud of fury and shoved Stew-Pot in the chest, hard, with both hands.

Everyone froze. This had never happened before. None of us were quite sure what came next.

Stew-Pot recovered first. He held out a hand. His friends stepped back. Then he walked up to where Darnell was still standing, stuck out his chest, and shoved him so hard Darnell fell to the ground.

Then I did a terrible thing. I did nothing. It was like my brain totally stopped and I couldn't move, because it didn't feel real. It was like something on TV. I just watched Stew-Pot. Like I said, fear can do strange things to people.

Stew-Pot was pacing back and forth, looking a little sweaty and worked up. He came over again and kicked Darnell, once, but really hard, in the stomach.

"Let that be a lesson, creep. Get out of here,"

Stew-Pot sneered. He snatched the lunch bag with the sandwich in it then nodded over his shoulder to his goons to let us through.

I helped Darnell up from the ground. I felt like yelling at him. I couldn't believe he had nearly let himself get killed over a stupid ham and Swiss sandwich. It wasn't the ham and Swiss, of course. It was Katrina Bixby and her stupid pep talk.

I let him lean on my shoulder and he limped the rest of the way to school. I couldn't think of anything else to say, so for once in my life I shut up. Darnell didn't look like he felt much like talking.

When we got inside the building, Darnell said, "I think I want to go see the nurse."

"Sure," I said.

She took one look at him and made him lie down.

Darnell turned over on his side and kind of folded himself up. I guess his stomach still really hurt.

"What happened to you?" Mrs. Addison asked.

I just gave Darnell a look like, *It's your call, D.* The grown-ups want to help, but sometimes telling on a bully like Stew-Pot can make life a whole lot worse.

Darnell said, "I must have eaten something, Mrs. A."

"Okay. Well, you lie there and see if you feel better in a little bit. Is your mom or dad at home?"

"My dad."

"Okay. Well, you lie there for now, and if you don't feel better soon, I'll call your dad to come pick you up."

Darnell nodded weakly.

Overhead, the bell rang. Great. I could imagine the glee on Mr. Jennings' face when he got to mark me late to Homeroom again, but really, that was the least of my problems.

"Are you going to be okay, D?" I asked softly.

Darnell nodded again and let out a little moan. He closed his eyes.

"Okay, I'll catch up with you later," I said. I shrugged on my backpack and stood there, twisting the straps. "I'd better be getting to class."

"Yeah," he said.

"I'm sorry," I said.

"Yeah," he said.

I felt awful. I just stood there the entire time, like an idiot. I am the worst best friend ever.

CHAPTER 11

Y ou can put away your books for today,"
Mr. Henley said, pulling down the screen
over the whiteboard. "Fluid dynamics is pretty
advanced, but since we recently finished up a
unit on weather, I thought you might be
interested in this." He walked to the back of the
room as he was talking and clicked off the
lights. The overhead projector whirred to life.

"2004, scientists see images from the Hubble

Space Telescope of swirling clouds of dust and gas around stars, and it reminds them of this famous painting." Mr. Henley fiddled with his laptop and we got fifteen seconds of deep space, followed by a swirly blue painting with yellow stars.

"Van Gogh's *Starry Night,*" Mr. Henley said proudly. "Painted by the artist Vincent Van Gogh in June of 1889 while he was in a mental asylum."

I actually know about Van Gogh. My mom told me when I was on one of my vegetable strikes that Van Gogh tried to live for a whole year on just bread and his teeth got all loose and started to fall out, so now I eat the pickles and other stuff Arlo puts on his hot dogs. You get to know a lot of strange things, being in my family.

"Okay, so what does this have to do with

fluid dynamics?" Mr. Henley asked. "Well, check out those swirls. Fluid dynamics is one of the great unsolved mysteries of science. The closest we've come to explaining turbulence is thanks to a mathematician named Andrey Kolmogorov. Yes, Katrina?"

"How do you spell his name?"

"K-O-L-M-O-G-O-R-O-V," Mr. Henley said. "He developed Kolmogorov scaling. Yes, Mike?"

Mikey had his hand in the air. "Uh, is this going to be on the test, Mr. Henley?"

"No," Mr. Henley said, "but someday you may realize that there are interesting things in life not directly related to your grade point average. SO, as I was saying." Mr. Henley clicked back to more space slides. "The picture I showed you from the Hubble Space Telescope got scientists thinking about Van Gogh. A team of physicists got together and used computers to analyze four of Van Gogh's paintings. What they found was that three of the paintings show Kolmogorov scaling. But the REALLY interesting part . . . ."

Mr. Henley clicked through a couple more slides to a painting with a man in a fur hat and coat with a bandage over his ear.

"This is one of Van Gogh's self-portraits," Mr. Henley said. "And yes, that is his ear, or rather *not* his ear. This was also painted in 1889, but in January when Van Gogh was being treated. Do you see the smoke curling up from the pipe he's smoking? Lots of twists and swirls, right? But not a match. Not like *Starry Night* and *Road with Cypress and Star* or *Wheat Field with Crows.* And the difference *seems* to be, that when Van Gogh was what we might call 'crazy,' he was able to accurately paint turbulence, something impossible for a human being without help from a computer."

I saw part of this movie once about Van Gogh and his brother late at night when my mom didn't know I was watching TV. Do you know who took care of everything while Van Gogh was being all crazy-genius? His brother, that's who. Van Gogh might be an amazing artist, but it's his brother I feel for. It isn't easy having a genius brother.

"Now I know none of you will," Mr. Henley said, writing on the whiteboard, "but there's a terrific TED talk on this subject by Natalya St. Clair, and if you watch it, and can prove to me you've watched it, I may just be so inclined to throw a couple of extra credit points your way."

The bell rang. We grabbed our backpacks and started filing out.

Mr. Henley called after us out the door,

"Don't forget to study for Thursday's test!"

Katrina caught up with me in the hall. She actually reached out and put one hand on my sleeve to get my attention. I knew we had clicked!

"Hey, Theo," she said, brushing her hair out of her face.

"Oh hey," I said, trying to think of something smarter and funnier to say than that.

"Darnell wasn't in class today," she said.

"Yeah," I said. "He wasn't feeling good. I think he went home early."

"Oh," she said. "That's too bad."

"Yeah," I agreed. She didn't know the half of it.

"We had talked about getting together to study for tomorrow's test," she said.

"Oh yeah, that would be really great!" I said.

She smiled. She's SO cute. "Great!" she said. "I'll text you later. Can you give me your number?"

She handed me her phone. For a microsecond, our hands touched. I was so jittery I had trouble entering the numbers. The whole time I was standing there I kept thinking, *I can't believe Katrina Bixby asked me for my number! How amazing is that!* WOW.

"Is your mom bringing something to the FunFest tomorrow?" she asked. "Darnell said she's like a food scientist or something."

He said what? Trust your best friend to welch on you for a pretty face!

"My mom's bringing vanilla cupcakes with strawberry frosting," Katrina said. "See you later, Theo!" And she was off, her long braid swinging down her back.

I think I tried to say, "Bye," or "See you

later," but nothing came out.

Way to go, Westly. So much for impressing her by being smart or funny. But it didn't matter, she totally liked me. I could tell.

CHAPTER 12

I was feeling so mixed up inside. I was pretty sure the cutest girl in the school liked me, but I had chickened out and let my best friend get kicked in the gut by a two-bit gangster-wanna-be and I still felt really bad about that.

I walked home slowly, kicking a rock along the sidewalk. My life was getting complicated and I had a lot to think about. After a while my foot started hurting. Real smart, Theo.

I turned the corner just past the Nesbitts' house where you can see through the alley over the backyard fences. There was a sort of green ooze, like marshmallow or shaving cream, coming out of our house. Einstein was standing in the backyard whining as the ooze pushed its way out through his pet door.

Oh great.

I grabbed onto my backpack and started running.

As I got close, I heard Grandma's voice saying, "Yee-hah!" followed by Toby's, "That was SO awesome, Grandma!"

More of the stuff was oozing out down the concrete steps, coiling and piling on top of itself. Einstein backed up several steps and started barking at it.

I took two seconds to pat Einstein on the head and tell him it was going to be all right, then I yanked open the back door. Big mistake. A giant wave of green goo came spewing out all over me. YUCK!

As it started to fizzle and collapse, I saw Grandma and Toby. They were wearing protective eyewear and rubber gloves and boots.

"Let's do it again, Grandma!" Toby said. "Pleeease?"

Actually it was only Grandma wearing lab goggles. Toby was wearing a pair of bright orange goggles Mom bought him for swim lessons. His rubber gloves went all the way up to his tiny armpits.

I was NOT wearing boots or protective gear, like a raincoat. My clothes were soaked. The warm soapy foam was in my hair and on my face. I felt it seeping into my sneakers as I stood there.

"WHAT was that?" I yelled.

"Elephant toothpaste!" said Toby, jumping up and down in his yellow rubber rain boots. "Mint-flavored!"

"What??"

Grandma pulled her goggles up on top of her head. "Just testing out a decomposition reaction."

"That's what makes all the bubbles!" Toby said. He picked up a huge handful of foam in his gloves to show me. "Mom has LOTS of potassium iodide," he said happily.

"*Has* or *had?*" I asked him.

Toby looked at the ceiling.

"Why is it green?" I asked Grandma, even though that really should have been the least of my worries.

"Food coloring, Theo," Grandma said, like it was the most obvious thing in the world. "Toby wanted peppermint flavor, to make it more realistic. Wouldn't taste it, though, if I were you," she added, as if I might actually do something that dumb.

"How are we going to get this cleaned up before Mom and Dad get home?" I groaned.

Grandma made a tsk-ing sound. "Hydrogen peroxide decomposes into water and oxygen, Theo. It's just water and dish soap now."

"But it's all over everything!" I objected.

"Yes, well," Grandma admitted. "The experiment did occur more rapidly than I anticipated. Think we can snake the garden hose in here through the back window?"

I peeled off my wet jacket and tossed it onto a kitchen chair. "I'll go get the mop."

Toby kept talking the entire time we were cleaning up. "Grandma says a large volume of oxygen molecules is produced in the experiment," he explained while I rummaged in the downstairs hall closet for a bucket. "That's what makes the foam shoot out so fast." He stopped suddenly. You could see a light bulb had just come on inside his head. "Grandma, could we use *highly concentrated* hydrogen peroxide to propel things, like a rocket?"

Toby is OBSESSED with rockets.

Grandma winked at him. "Let's find out!"

"Don't even think about it!" I told them both sternly.

In the end, there was just one large green stain we couldn't get out of the carpet, but we moved the rug from upstairs down to the front hall to cover it.

Grandma pulled off her rubber gloves. "The rug looks better here anyway," she said.

Toby turned to me and asked, "Would I like to see a naked egg?"

CHAPTER 13

I don't know, would you?" I said automatically. "Wait, what? That sounds really gross."

"You soaked the egg in vinegar to dissolve the calcium carbonate of the shell. They get all rubbery. They *look* like they can be bounced, but the membrane is actually quite fragile," he added sadly.

I was about to ask where exactly he had been

testing this out, but Toby's mouth kept running.

"You have a germ garden. Would I like to see your germ garden? I have to be careful handling the bags. The instructions say NOT to open them, because certain types of mold can cause allergic reactions."

"Okay, that is *not* normal," I told him. "Do you have any idea how weird and creepy you are? I'm going upstairs to take a shower. And no more experiments while I'm gone," I warned.

Toby and Grandma looked very solemn, but in a silly way.

"I mean it," I said. "I don't have time to clean up any more disasters. I've got a science test to study for and homework to do tonight."

By the time I came downstairs again, Mom was home from work and Grandma was sitting in the living room on the sofa with Einstein stretched out on the floor in front of her.

"Where's Toby?" I asked, immediately suspicious.

"Even geniuses need naps," said Grandma. "Especially geniuses." She was studying her latch hook pattern and looking for the right color yarn.

"What's this one going to be?" I asked.

"I thought I'd try a tiger this time, dear," said Grandma. "Have a seat," she suggested.

I thought about getting out my Science book to study, but I just didn't have the energy.

"How was school today?" Grandma asked.

I stretched out on the sofa next to her and leaned over the side to scratch Einstein's head. He shut his eyes and yawned.

"School was okay, I guess," I said.

"But?" she said gently.

I sighed. "There's this jerk who takes

Darnell's sandwich every morning on the way to school and today Darnell was dumb enough to try to fight him. It didn't work out so well."

"Well dear," Grandma said, frowning at her latch hook. "You could always poison him."

She really scares me sometimes.

"Uh, I think I'll go see what Mom's making for dinner," I said.

"Good luck," Grandma called after me. "Now, which shade of orange do you suppose is Atomic Tangerine?"

I wandered into the kitchen where Mom was making dinner. Since Darnell went home from school early, I hadn't gotten any fast food this afternoon. I was starving.

The trick with Mom's dinners sometimes is to get to the ingredients before she has time to combine them. I started noshing my way along the counter: ham, cheese cubes, croutons. I even nibbled a little bit of raw broccoli, although in general I try to avoid eating things that are green. Mom's experiments with green bean ice cream at the July 4th picnic last summer only confirmed that.

When I was pretty sure Mom was distracted, I asked, very by-the-way, "So Mom, you know about that food for the FunFest Bake-Off? What about asking Mrs. Bixby? I bet she has some good recipes."

Mom squinted at the notes she had made in her cookbook. Honestly, I think I saw some chemical equations in there. "Mrs. Bixby?" she said.

"Katrina's mom. Katrina says her mom is bringing vanilla cupcakes with strawberry frosting for the FunFest tomorrow. Doesn't that sound nice?"

"Oh Theo," Mom said, in that sad, disappointed tone she uses on Einstein when he tracks mud into the living room. "Don't be boring."

"What is this?" I asked. It looked like a lot of white rubber bands floating in a bowl of ice water.

"Calamari," Mom said.

"What's that?"

"Squid," Dad said, coming into the kitchen through the back door from the garage. "Mmm. In some cultures it's considered a delicacy." He reached into the bowl and picked up one of the rubber bands and dropped it into his open mouth.

"Yuck! Dad! You just ate that thing raw!" I said.

"Yup." He leaned over my head to kiss my mom. With squid lips. GROSS.

"Hey, Dad," I said brightly. "Maybe *you* could make something for the school FunFest this year. Like Darnell's dad is. That would be cool, right?"

Dad frowned thoughtfully and pushed his glasses up further on his nose. The frames broke on one side a couple months ago, and he wrapped them in duct tape to hold them together, but they've never sat quite right on his face since. Duct tape. So lame.

"Well," he said hesitantly. "Your mom is the food expert, Theo."

Grandma appeared in the doorway, wispy white hair floating gently out of her bun. "Has anyone seen the baking soda?" she asked.

CHAPTER 14

Grandma looked around the kitchen. "I wonder where it could be," she said.

"Does anyone else want to know why Grandma is looking for the baking soda?" I asked when she had gone.

"Now, Theo," said Mom, looking down through her glasses at me. "Sometimes elderly people get confused. You can't sit on the sidelines of life, Theo, being boring, being theoretical," Mom continued. This is one of my mom's favorite lectures. "You have to get out there, push the envelope, experiment!"

"Yes, but do you have to make other people eat your experiments?" I said under my breath.

There was a noise from the pantry and Grandma's voice said cheerfully, "Never mind!"

"Where's Toby?" I asked suddenly.

But now Dad was off and running. He hadn't taken his jacket off yet. I think he had forgotten he still had it on. "You know, I've never really tried to bake before, but, come to think of it, a lot of cakes today, particularly the kind you see at weddings, are works of engineering. I mean, fondant, plaster of paris, cardboard struts. I wonder if I could build a bridge out of cake blocks. Do you have a piece of scratch paper, Zee?" He whisked his mechanical pencil out of his shirt pocket and clicked the end several times.

I was starting to think this was a bad idea. I mean, yes, technically you can get *food grade* plaster of paris, but Mom says calcium sulfate is also used in drywall, make-up, and orthopedic casts, and do you really want to be eating something that can do all that?

Just then Grandma stuck her head in the kitchen again. I'm pretty sure I saw a box of baking soda behind her back. "I could always make something for the FunFestival," she suggested.

"No!" all three of us said together, although to be fair, my parents said it a lot more nicely and from better motives.

"Suit yourselves," Grandma said. And then, "Do we have anything larger than a 9-volt battery in the house?"

"You know what I can never find enough of," Dad said to Mom, "is wire hangers."

"Aren't plastic ones just as good?" my mom asked. She had pulverized the croutons and was dredging the rubber bands in egg yolk.

"I suppose so, but we used to have a lot of the wire ones in the upstairs closet." He shrugged. I could tell in the back of his mind he was still thinking about the tensile strength of cake bricks.

"Where did you say Toby was?" I asked.

"Why are you looking for Toby?" my mom said, finally asking a relevant question.

I thought about saying, "To warn him about the calamari," but I knew that would get me in trouble, so instead I said, "He was asking me earlier about my Snap Circuits LIGHT set. I thought I'd let him play with it."

This was an outright lie. I would never let

Genius Baby get anywhere *close* to my Snap Circuits.

"Oh Honey, that's really sweet!" Mom gave me a huge, happy smile. "Toby is Very Special. It's not easy for him to make friends of his own. I know how much he wants to play with you and Darnell."

Just then, there was a big POP and all the lights in the house went out.

CHAPTER 15

S hucks," said my dad. "Probably another fuse."

"Maybe a tree branch fell on one of the power lines, that can happen," Mom suggested. "Roger, Honey, would you hand me one of the flashlights in that drawer there?"

"Fuses go out all the time in these old houses," Dad said.

Yeah, in *our* house especially.

There was a click and a little round circle of light appeared. Dad handed the flashlight to Mom.

"Maybe we should look into getting a generator. What do you think, Honey?" Mom called over her shoulder as Dad went clomping down the basement stairs.

"I don't think that's necessary," I said hastily. "I mean, what's the occasional power outage here or there? Cozy, right?"

Who knows what Grandma and Toby could get up to with their very own generator!

"So," I said cheerfully, "I guess this means take-out for dinner, huh?"

"It does not." Mom had to take the small flashlight from between her teeth to answer me. "Thank goodness the hand-held immersion blender your father gave me last year for Christmas is battery-operated. How lucky is that?"

"Um, so what is it exactly you're making for dinner tonight?"

"Well," said Mom.

This is never a good beginning.

"It's like . . . ." She paused, searching for words.

Also not a good sign.

"Well, it's like a ham and broccoli bake, but with a few other ingredients. Like a Ham-Broccoli-Cheddar Gratin Surprise."

A lot of my mom's recipes end in *Surprise*. Ugh. I'd to have to eat *two* cheeseburgers tomorrow, maybe three, to make up for today.

"And the surprise part is?" I asked, not really wanting to know. It's like one of those horrible accidents where you want to look, but at the same time you don't want to look.

"The seafood, of course," Mom said. And

then added, "Also the grapes."

Ick. "Anyone dumb enough to eat it is sure going to be surprised," I muttered under my breath.

Mom whipped around and dazzled me with the flashlight. Mom may not have taste buds, but her hearing is really, really good. They say when one sense goes, the others get stronger. It has to do with something called neuroplasticity. Dad told me about it once.

"Don't you have a science test to study for, Mister?" Mom asked pointedly.

In the dark? But I knew better than to mess with Mom when she was in one of her moods. Besides, it was true. I did.

By the time Dad got the lights back on, Grandma was in her usual spot on the sofa with her latch hook. Her hair looked a little frizzled around the edges, but then it usually does. I eyed her suspiciously. She didn't even blink.

Toby wandered into the living room a minute later with his hair all messed up like he had been taking a nap or in contact with high voltage. He climbed up onto the sofa next to Grandma. I thought he had a sort of dark smudge over one eye, but then Mom stuck her head out of the kitchen to ask, "If pecan sandies are made with pecans, do you suppose I could make cookies out of other tree nuts, like acorns?" and when I looked back at Toby, the smudge was gone and he and Grandma had innocent expressions.

CHAPTER 16

I was still waiting for a text from Katrina so we could study together for the science test tomorrow, but I figured I'd better get started on my other homework, so after dinner I hauled my backpack up to my room and drug out my math book. I flipped it open and read:

Paul lives in Buffalo, which is 285 kilometers from Pittsburgh, and 1,841 kilometers closer than Maria lives in Denver. If Paul and Maria meet in Pittsburgh, how many miles

Who is Maria, and why does she want to meet Paul in Pittsburgh? Why not Philadelphia, or even Chicago? And what kind of loser boyfriend is Paul that he won't pop for a plane ticket to Denver? This was clearly a job for Genius Baby.

"Hey, Toby," I yelled. "What's 285 plus 1,841 kilometers, in miles?" I hope Paul at least sprung for flowers after making Maria schlep halfway across the country.

Toby wandered into my room, dragging what he calls his Wubbie. He said, "1,321." I can't believe Mom still lets him sleep with that disgusting blanket. It's been through the wash so many times that it's starting to look like the towel Mom keeps by the back door for Einstein when he comes in from outside, and isn't four a little old for a security blanket anyway? But if

Toby was giving me answers, I wasn't about to get on his case.

"Thanks, little man." I quickly wrote the answer down on my paper. "Hey, if a forty-five-ounce jar of tomato sauce costs $2.98 and serves ten, and a two-pound box of spaghetti costs $2.28 and serves sixteen, and Louise has ten dollars, how many friends can she invite to her dinner party?"

"TO-BY," Dad called from downstairs. "Bath time."

Like he was delivering the most important news in the world, Toby announced, "Daddy will take you a bath now."

"It's 'give,' moron," I said. "You *take* baths. Daddy *gives* you one. And you're supposed to say *me,* not *you* when you talk about yourself."

Toby stuck his tongue out at me.

I could hear Dad saying, "Where is Toby?

Go get him, Einstein," and Einstein came clattering up the stairs and nosed his way in.

"Wait!" I yelled. "Hang on, Dad! Quick Toby, how many people can Louise invite?"

Toby smiled. "Daddy will take you a bath now."

"Arrrgg!" I put my head down on my desk. Great, now Louise won't be able to have her spaghetti party. I hope Dad realizes he's ruined her social life.

I tried working on the problem by myself, but pretty soon I started wondering if maybe Louise should throw in some garlic bread and a side salad, possibly with a dessert at the end, like chocolate cake. This was going nowhere. Clearly, extreme hunger had affected my brain. I closed my Math book and went downstairs to see if I could find something edible in our fridge.

On my way to the kitchen, I passed the living room and looked in.

"Hey, Grandma," I said.

She was frowning at two tiny pieces of yarn. "Why do they have to make tan and light brown so close in color?" she asked. "Don't they know old people do these things?"

My phone dinged. The text from Katrina!

CHAPTER 17

I quickly checked my messages: *How is D?*

Fine, no thanks to you, I wanted to say. If Darnell hadn't developed some abnormal hero complex all of a sudden, none of this would have happened, but I texted: *Ok can u study?*

I saw Grandma watching me over the rim of her glasses, pretending not to. I fidgeted. Then: *R u @ abb is D there?*

What? *No,* I texted back. And then added:

Can u study?

My heart ticked the seconds. Finally: *Not 2nite.*

Well, she could have said that to begin with.

"Everything okay?" Grandma asked. "You look down."

I was so depressed, I didn't bother to lie. "There's this awesomely cute girl in my class who likes me, and we were supposed to study together, and now she just totally blew me off. I don't get it."

"Well dear," Grandma said. "It sounds like she doesn't like you that much."

"Oh great, thanks a lot, Grandma! Way to cheer me up."

Grandma shrugged.

Toby padded into the living room in his pajamas. His hair was sticking up again but this time because it was still wet after his bath. He had his wubbie under one arm and his bedtime reading under the other. He held out the book to Grandma.

Grandma put down her latch hook tiger. "Robert Goddard and rockets again, eh?" she asked. "All right. Climb on up."

I looked over at Toby's sippy cup. "WHAT is he drinking?"

"Fake blood, dear," Grandma said calmly.

"That's SO revolting!" I said. "What's in it?"

Toby pulled the sippy cup out of his mouth. "Chocolate syrup. Also some corn syrup and red food coloring."

"That sounds like a lot of sugar for someone your age," I said. "Don't you know all that stuff will rot your teeth?"

Toby just pulled the sippy cup out again and said, "BLOOOOD," in his creepiest voice.

"Now where were we?" Grandma asked. She

tilted her glasses forward to see better as she opened the book. "Goddard was a man ahead of his time. Did you know he came up with the idea of a space probe like Voyager in 1920, when most scientists still thought a rocket couldn't fly through the vacuum of outer space? He wasn't too much older than you, Theo, when he had his vision for a spacecraft capable of reaching Mars. It set him off on his quest."

"Okay, okay, I get it!" I grumbled. "I'm not a genius like Toby or Robert Goddard!"

"I never said that," Grandma replied.

"We can't ALL be geniuses," I said.

"Of course not," Grandma said as she thumbed through the pages. "Someone has to pick up the pieces." She looked at me through her thick glasses and she smiled. "So much like your grandfather. He was a dear man." She winked at me. "Used to let him cheat off my science tests because he was so cute!"

"EEW! Grandma! I did NOT need to know that."

"Wasn't old forever you know," Grandma said. Then she looked at me severely, just like my mom does when she's giving me one of her lectures. "Science is about trial-and-error, Theo! Taking chances, not being afraid to sometimes look foolish, make a little mess, or make mistakes so you can learn from them."

"Make a little mess?" I said. *"Little?* You mean like the time we had to take Dad's glue gun over to Mrs. Crowley's to fix her brass chandelier?"

"She was very nice about it," Grandma said primly.

"Yeah! Because she's super old and mostly blind!"

"Perhaps we should have aimed our

electromagnetic pipe gun farther from her house," Grandma admitted. "But to be fair, she shouldn't leave her dining room windows open. Let me see. Ah, here we go. *Methods of Detecting and Measuring Gaseous Rebound,"* she read.

Toby snuggled closer to her on the sofa and tucked his smelly blanket under his cheek.

Mom came in holding one of her food science textbooks under her arm. "Did you know the Australian chef Adam Melonas is famous for making octopus popsicles using transglutaminase and an orange-saffron gel made from seaweed extract?"

We all stared at her.

"I'll be downstairs in the basement," Mom said.

Even Grandma and Toby looked alarmed.

"Don't you have homework to do, Theo?"

Mom asked me, then disappeared.

"Transglutaminase is another word for 'meat glue,' isn't it?" I asked.

"Yes," Toby and Grandma said at the same time.

I put my head in my hands.

Grandma said briskly, "You know, I think I might like to go to this FunFair of yours."

I groaned, my head still buried in my hands. "Fun*Fest,* Grandma, Fun*Fest.* And why not? What's one more person witnessing my total humiliation tomorrow?"

"Wonder where my hat with the sunflowers went," Grandma said. Grandma has more hats with fake flowers than anyone I know. Some of them have feathers, or fake fruit, but mostly they're flowers. Fortunately she doesn't go out much anymore.

"I know it's around here somewhere,"

Grandma was muttering. She put down the Goddard book and shuffled toward the open basement door. "Zee?" she called down. "Do you know where my hat with the sunflowers is?"

"What, Mom?"

"My hat, with the sunflowers, dear. I'm sure it's in one of those hat boxes in the attic." All of our storage is in the attic. The basement is full of Mom's lab.

"Would I like to read to you?" Toby asked hopefully.

I didn't even have the heart to say, "I don't know, would you?" I just said. "Yeah, okay."

It was just as well Katrina blew me off because starting tomorrow I was about to be a complete and utter loser forever.

CHAPTER 18

I woke up again before my alarm went off.
Thursday.

I had been so sure I'd be able to think of something in time to stop Mom, like I bragged to Darnell, but the clock had run out and I still had nothing. I felt sick to my stomach.

At least I'd had an idea for how to fix things for Darnell. My life may have been over, I thought as I finished brushing my teeth, but I could still come through for best friend.

Dad had already left for work. Grandma and Toby were sitting at the breakfast table in the kitchen when I came downstairs.

Mom wandered into the kitchen with a cup of coffee in one hand and a pencil stuck behind her ear.

"Uh, I thought you were going to work this morning," I said.

"Oh," Mom said cheerfully. "I decided to take the whole day off so I could really concentrate on baking."

Yup, dead man walking.

"I don't feel so good," I said. It was kind of true, plus stomachache is always a good excuse in our house. "Maybe I should stay home today."

Mom reached out and ruffled my hair sympathetically.

"Mom!" I jerked away.

Bad move. Mom put her hands on her hips. "You look fine to me, mister." *Nuts.* I always forget I've got to lead up to these things. Moan and groan a little bit, lie on the sofa and cough.

Toby snickered and I glared at him. Little brothers can be such a pain.

"Hey wait," I said to Mom. It should have occurred to me before, but I had been distracted by thinking up my Master Plan to save Darnell. "If you're going to be at the FunFest this afternoon, and Grandma's also coming, who's going to watch Toby?"

"My friend Mrs. McKinney is going to watch him for the day," Grandma said. She held her hand over the top of her glass as Mom passed by. "No thank you, dear, no celery juice for me."

I was so shocked, I grasped the less

important part first. "You have a friend??"

"Of course, dear," Grandma said, a bit stiffly.

"How come I didn't know you have a friend?"

"Well Theo, I imagine there are many things you don't know," Grandma said tartly.

"Isn't it wonderful?" my mom gushed. "And at the last minute! I don't know what we would have done if Grandma's friend hadn't come to the rescue. I suppose Toby would have had to come to the FunFest with us!"

"Uh, yeah, sure. That's okay then," I said. Toby let loose at the FunFest sounded like a bad idea. Besides, I was pressed for time this morning. "I'm, um, just going to make my lunch," I said. "In the basement. Bye."

"I thought he bought his lunch at school," I heard Mom say to Grandma.

I grabbed a couple of cans from the pantry, a

jar of mayo from the fridge, some salt and pepper, and went down to the lab. I looked around.

"Hey, does anybody know where we keep the stearic acid?" I called up the stairs.

Mom's voice filtered down from above. "Look on the shelf next to the thermal immersion circulator, left-hand side." My parents are WAY too trusting.

I needed a couple of other ingredients, but it didn't take long. When I was done, I carefully screwed on the lid to seal the jar. Now all I had to do was make sure it got into my backpack safely with no one looking. I should have brought my backpack down with me, but that definitely would have looked suspicious.

When I came upstairs from the lab, Grandma was gone. Mom was reading her dog-eared copy of Belle Lowe's *Experimental Cookery* to

Toby and finishing her breakfast. Mom's a big believer in the four food groups, so she adds peas to the sliced banana on her cereal. Ick. I bet Katrina's mom never does anything weird like that.

Einstein, of course, could smell the tuna fish salad on me right away. He pricked up his ears.

Toby immediately looked up alertly.

I needed cover.

CHAPTER 19

Fortunately, just then we heard Grandma call downstairs, "I'm almost sure it was in one of these hatboxes up here."

"Oh my goodness!" Mom exclaimed. "Mom! What are you doing in the attic?"

"Looking for my hat, dear," Grandma's voice said. "You know, the one with the sunflowers on it. I wanted to wear it to little Theo's FunTime this afternoon."

"Hang on, Mom," my mother called. "I'll be right up." She had her finger in the index and was flipping through pages in the huge book.

I stood on one foot. "Uh, Mom?"

"I particularly wanted to wear that hat," Grandma said from upstairs.

"Could I get into trouble if—?"

"Yes," Mom said. "If you have to ask, the answer is probably yes. Why?"

"Uh, no reason."

Mom stopped what she was doing and looked at me closely. "You can always talk to me or to your father if you need to, you know that, right?" She reached out to ruffle my hair again and thought better of it. She called upstairs, "Don't worry, I'll help you look for your hat, Mom. I'm sure we'll find it." She winked at me. My mom is such a sweet person. She has no idea Grandma has almost blown up the house several times with her crazy science experiments. "Well, I better go upstairs and help your grandma in the attic," Mom said. "Do you have your lunch money?"

I patted my empty pocket. "Yeah, Mom."

"Are you sure you don't want breakfast? I can whip up a peanut butter-and-jelly yogurt you can take with you," Mom offered.

"Uh, no, I'm really not that hungry," I said, thinking of the egg and cheese breakfast burrito Darnell had waiting for me.

"Okay. I'll see you this afternoon, huh?" Mom said happily, pulling a bunch of spinach out of the refrigerator.

I picked up my backpack. I knew it wouldn't do any good, but I tried one more time. I cleared my throat.

"Uh, what are you thinking of bringing to the FunFest today?" I asked.

"I haven't made up my mind," Mom said in her thoughtful, dreamy, absent-minded scientist way. "Maybe something with asparagus? I'm out of octopus, but there are those cans of eel in the pantry that ought to be used sometime soon. Maybe something with that? Then again, I woke up in the middle of the night with a really creative idea for donuts, so that's a possibility too."

DOOM.

Mom pulled her head out of the refrigerator and smiled at me. "Don't worry, Theo," she reassured me. "It'll be delicious, whatever it is. Have a good day at school!"

I laughed hollowly.

Einstein was still following me around. At the door, I turned and told him to stay. "I promise, if I survive today, I'll open a can of tuna just for you when I get home," I told him.

"In the meantime, just try to keep an eye on things, okay? You really let me down yesterday with the green sludge, pal."

Einstein whined.

"I hear you, buddy," I said. When Toby and Grandma get a crazy idea into their heads, no force on earth can stop them.

Just as I was about to open the front door, the doorbell rang, and I nearly jumped out of my skin. I turned the latch and opened the door.

I don't know what I had been expecting. Mary Poppins? Mrs. McKinney was large and old and ugly.

"Uh," I stammered.

"Mrs. McKinney," she said, in a thick, grim Scottish voice that could peel paint off the walls.

"Hey, Mom," I gulped. "Mrs. McKinney's here."

"I'll be right there!" Mom called brightly.

Toby had let himself down from the breakfast table and padded over to where he could see the door. I saw Mrs. McKinney look him up and down in a way that made me think she didn't think much of little boys, even if they were geniuses.

"Whoops, gotta go," I said and slid past Mrs. McKinney.

Darnell was waiting outside for me.

Mrs. Crowley, who lives in the house on our right, had just opened her door and was bending over to pick up the newspaper on her porch. She straightened up with the rolled newspaper in her hand.

I shouted "Morning, Mrs. Crowley!" to her at the top of my lungs as I jogged down the front steps.

She squinted in my direction and smiled and

nodded her head up and down. On top of being very near-sighted, she is also mostly deaf. We are very lucky to have her for a neighbor.

CHAPTER 20

Give me your sandwich," I said as soon as Darnell and I had turned the corner.

"Why? What do you want it for?" Darnell asked suspiciously.

"Trust me. Just give it to me." I knelt on the ground and opened it up. "Mmm, Turkey-Bacon Club. Here," I said, handing him a couple slices of turkey and one of the sticks of bacon. No point in wasting good food. I ate the other stick of bacon and the rest of the turkey, carefully setting aside the lettuce and tomato on the grass.

"What are you doing??" Darnell watched me take out the jar from my backpack and remove the lid.

I started scooping the mixture out and spreading it on the pretzel bread roll, the kind where the outside is a smooth, lovely dark brown and the inside is soft and chewy.

"I can't tell you," I said.

"Why not?"

"Plausible deniability," I said. "I heard that on a TV show once." I carefully laid down the leaf of lettuce and replaced the sliced tomato. Perfect. It was a real shame about the pretzel roll, but in the battle between Good and Evil, you have to be prepared to make some sacrifices.

"What is it?" Darnell asked, sounding worried.

"I have two words for you, my friend," I said. "Tuna Fish Surprise."

"That's three words," Darnell said.

I rolled my eyes. "Work with me here! I'm trying to help you out. Where did the plastic wrap go?" We carefully rewrapped the sandwich and nestled it back into its brown paper bag home. Torpedo One, locked and loaded.

Darnell kept shaking his head as we walked along. "I'm pretty sure whatever this is, it's a bad idea."

"C'mon, D! Where's your sense of curiosity and adventure? Your scientific inquiry? Is this the kind of can-do spirit that put a man on the moon?"

"No."

"All right then," I said, as if that settled it.

"I still don't think it's a good idea, messing with Stew-Pot," Darnell mumbled.

"Stop being so negative, D. You're making me nervous."

Darnell looked so much like Einstein for a moment with his large, sad eyes that I tried to cheer him up.

"Look," I said. "It's like at the end of the tournament in Book 4 where Harry and Cedric are getting ready to go up against Voldemort and Harry says—"

"You mean the fight when Voldemort kills Cedric and Harry can't save him?" Darnell interrupted.

I started over. "Um. Well, like in Book 2 then, with Ron and the giant spiders . . . ." But it was too late.

Stew-Pot walked up to us slowly, pounding

one fist into his other cupped hand.

"What's it going to be today?" He jerked his head at Darnell. "You gonna go all tough guy on me again, creep?"

It wasn't cold, but Darnell was shivering.

I spoke up. "No, sir. We learned our lesson. We're ready to cooperate today."

Stew-Pot fell back. "Search his pockets, Mikey."

Mikey lumbered over, looking like The Thing in the Fantastic Four, but less cuddly.

"Did you know denser bodies displace more water?" I asked. My mouth was starting to run all by itself again, which is usually when I get into trouble. "Mr. Henley says if something is heavy enough, it can actually bend space-time. Hey, look, my watch slowed!"

Mikey accidentally-on-purpose elbowed me.

"Ouch! Go easy on me, you big oaf!" I said.

Mikey straightened up. Isn't there a height and weight restriction, like, you must be less than this tall to be in the fifth grade?

"Hey," Mikey said. "He called me an orf!"

"I called you an oaf, Dumb-head," I said. "It's in the dictionary. Look it up." I really could have come up with something better than dumb-head, but the adrenaline was messing with my head.

"Shut up, Westly," Stew-Pot snapped.

I get told that a lot.

Mikey finished his search. "He's clean."

"Everybody happy now?" I grumbled, shoving my pockets back into place.

Then Mikey turned toward Darnell and everyone held their breath. Except for Darnell. I don't think he was breathing at all.

I nudged him. "Give him the sandwich, D," I said out of the corner of my mouth.

CHAPTER 21

Darnell held out the brown paper sack.

Mikey took it to Stew-Pot.

Stew-Pot slid the sandwich out and carefully unwrapped it. He walked up really close, like less than a foot from Darnell's face and took a huge bite. He just stood there, chewing, tearing into the pretzel bread roll with his teeth.

"Mmm," he said. "This tastes SO good."

I opened my mouth again. I was about to say,

"That's because my mom makes her own homemade mayo," but then I remembered the sandwich was supposed to be Darnell's.

Stew-Pot gave me a suspicious look. "What's with you, weirdo?"

"Nothing. Not a thing. Everything's fine. Go right ahead. Enjoy. Is it a good sandwich?" I closed my mouth to make myself stop talking.

It was too late to anyway. Stew-Pot was licking mayonnaise off his lips.

"Something funny, Westly?"

"Nope. Not at all. Perhaps Darnell and I had better be moving along," I suggested.

Stew-Pot was still eyeing me. He licked his fingers and nodded to the human barricade to let us through.

Darnell didn't look back until we reached school. He just kept shaking his head. "Oh man, tomorrow we are so dead."

"I've got bigger problems," I said. This afternoon was the FunFest, and I still had no idea what horrible food experiment Mom was bringing.

"Please put your books away and take out a Number Two pencil," Mr. Henley said.

Cripes! I had completely forgotten about studying for the science test.

Mr. Henley walked through the aisles, handing out copies of the test upside down. I turned around and gave Darnell a grin and quick thumbs up for good luck.

"You may now turn over your tests," Mr. Henley said.

At the top of the test, Mr. Henley had written, *Take your time as you work through the items on the test. Show all your work for the short answers, and remember physics is phun!!*

Seriously, why do adults even bother trying to be funny?

I read the first question:

1. Which of the following groups of materials could be used to build an electromagnet?

    A. Aluminum wire, plastic rod, battery

    B. Copper wire, iron nail, battery

    C. Bare wire, metal paper clip, magnet

    D. Insulated wire, battery, light bulb

"Mr. Henley."

"Yes, Stewart?"

"Can I go to the bathroom?" Stew-Pot was groaning and holding his stomach.

I knew the answer to Question One. You have to use wire metal coat hangers if you are building a secret giant electromagnet in your basement. Plastic doesn't conduct electricity, so that ruled out answer B. Okay, so maybe something good had come out of whatever Grandma and Toby were doing in our basement that night. Even if it had meant eating Ham-Broccoli-Cheddar Gratin Surprise by candlelight. Then again, eating one of Mom's dinners in the dark might be for the best. On to the next question.

> 2. Juanita uses a catapult to launch the five objects shown in the table below. Assuming the catapult launches each object with the same amount of force each time, which object do you predict will move the fastest when launched?

Juanita and my brother Toby should really get together. Or maybe not. Maybe we should keep them as far apart as possible! See? This is why I stink at word problems. I always go for the human angle. Focus, Theo, focus! Okay.

I reread the question. Wait, I know this one. I remembered. Lighter objects go up faster. Score!

I flexed my fingers. I was on a roll. Come on, Number Two pencil, don't fail me now.

"Hey, Mr. Henley."

"Yes, Stewart?"

"I'm not feeling so good. Can I have a pass to go to the bathroom again?"

I kept going. All right, I admit, I totally guessed on some of them, but I know I got the one on plankton right.

19. When a liquid is heated, what processes is responsible for changing liquid into a gas?

A. Precipitation

B. Condensation

C. Transpiration

D. Evaporation

What was it Grandma had said when she was explaining the fog machine to Darnell? Arrrgg! I tried to picture the backyard filled with smoke, Grandma in her flower-print dress, the breathing mask pushed back up on top of her wispy white hair. I thought super, super hard. I could hear Grandma's voice saying in my head, "When it's heated, the glycerin and water evaporate and turn into gas." Evaporate! YES!!! Thank you, Grandma!

Five questions left.

20. Linus observes a gas is formed when a liquid reacts with a catalyst. The chemical reaction Linus is seeing take place when one substance breaks down into two or more substances is called:

A. double replacement.

B. splitting.

C. decomposition.

D. combination.

"Uh, Mr. Henley."

"Yes, Mr. Potts?" And you could tell from the way Mr. Henley said it, very slowly, that he was losing his patience.

"I really need to go to the bathroom."

"One last time, Stewart. If you need to go

again, I'm sending you to the nurse and you can complete a make-up test next Monday."

As he passed my desk, Stew-Pot leaned over and said in a nasty whisper, "I'm on to you, punk."

It was Darnell's sandwich. How come *I* get blamed for everything? But I kept my mouth shut. You can get in trouble for talking during a test.

"Eyes front, Mike Vickers, on your own test," Mr. Henley said. Boy, he was in a bad mood today.

I looked back at Question Twenty. I was having trouble and time was nearly up.

CHAPTER 22

Okay, so it probably wasn't combination because this was about breaking things down. I crossed off D. Probably not double replacement either. That left splitting and decomposition. In my mind I could see the green foam pushing through Einstein's pet door, spilling down over the steps into the backyard. *Think, Theo!* I *know* Grandma told me this one.

I grabbed my pencil in desperation and marked C. They say when you're not sure, go with C anyway, right? I could ask Grandma about it tonight. It would be too late then, but for now that was my best guess, and it was just going to have to do.

I put on the gas and got through the last five questions about ecosystems and inherited traits. I wrote down my last answer and flipped to the last page.

EXTRA CREDIT +2

What is the name of the statistical model used to analyze turbulence?

The bell rang and Mr. Henley said, "Pencils down, everybody. Turn in your tests."

I quickly scrawled *Kallmegorbachev* and hoped that was close enough.

"How do you think you did?" I asked Darnell when we were out in the hall.

Darnell said, "Okay, I guess. Man! What did you do to Stew-Pot?"

"Oh hey, Katrina," I said. I was trying to be all cool and stuff, so I sort of tossed my head to sweep the hair out of my eyes when she walked over to us. Time for a touch of the ol' Westly charm. "How's it going?"

"Hey, Darnell," she said. "I got your note. It was really sweet. I like you too."

Wait, what note? Why am I always the last to know things around here?

After eighth period, we all trooped into the gym where the FunFest was being set up. The gym was blocked off in sections with hay bales for games, food, and a place to buy school spirit stuff. Up on stage, the band kids were sitting down and taking out their instruments. Mr. Henley was standing at the microphone at the front of the stage, telling parents how to string colored lights around bundles of corn stalks.

I craned my head and looked around the gym. "Do you see my mom or grandma?" I asked Darnell.

"No, but there's my dad." He pointed.

We walked across the gym to where the food tables were going up. Darnell's dad was laying out a plastic yellow tablecloth over the fold-out table.

"Chocolate Éclair Bombs?" I asked hopefully.

"Yes, you can have one," Arlo said. "But just one, Theo," he shook his finger at me and chuckled. He knows me too well.

"Yeah, yeah," I said. "Thanks, Mr. Samuels."

Darnell and I both helped ourselves to the puff pastry drizzled with chocolate icing.

Mmm. I would totally live on Mr. Samuels' éclairs forever if I could. One bite through the flaky outer layer and you're into the pastry cream in the middle, and I mean the real deal pastry cream made from milk and sugar and eggs, not the fake stuff where vegetable shortening gets whipped with thickeners like maltodextrin and emulsifiers like sodium stearoyl lactylate to make snack cakes that are "shelf-stable."

I automatically started to reach for another one and then stopped. Yup, there was Grandma in her hat with the huge sunflowers. She had forgotten to put in her teeth, so her mouth was all puckered in. She was holding an ugly old handbag in both hands and standing, looking lost and out of place, next to my mom, who was bending over one of the tables. Time to discover what my mom spent the morning cooking up in her lab. My heart dropped into my shoes.

CHAPTER 23

U h, hey, Mom. Hey, Grandma," I said as I came over. The metal serving trays had lids on them, so I couldn't see what was inside.

"Hello, Theo," my mom said happily. "How was your day?"

"All right, I guess," I mumbled. "I think I did kind of okay on the science test today."

Grandma just smiled behind her big, thick glasses.

A pretty woman started setting up at the table next to ours. She was wearing a pink dress with a short skirt and white heels, the kind of outfit my mom would never wear in a million years. She started unpacking row after row of pretty cupcakes topped with swirls of pink frosting. There were even tiny pink and purple flowers on top.

Katrina came up to the table and dropped her backpack. "Hi, Mom," she said.

Of course.

"Oh hi, Theo!" Katrina said.

This was epically bad. Any minute now everybody at my school was going to be whispering about what mom had brought to the FunFest. Asparagus pudding cups? Powdered jellyfish donuts? Fried eel skin fritters on a stick with strawberry-mayo dipping sauce? And Katrina and her perfect mom were going to be there, watching the whole catastrophe from front-row seats. My mind was racing. I wondered if I could squish myself into my locker, make a run for the gym exit, hide out in a bathroom stall until it the worst of it was over. *Go away,* I beamed at Katrina mentally. *Go away.*

Mrs. Bixby leaned over toward my mom and said, with just a hint of a Southern drawl, "I'm Patty Bixby. Are you Theo's mom?"

"Zenobia Westly," my mom said, extending her hand. This was very bad. When my mom likes someone right away, she'll add, "but you can call me, 'Zee,'" and she hadn't.

Mom seemed to have taken an instant dislike to Mrs. Bixby and her pretty-in-pink personality. So instead she said, like she was trying to remember something in one of her old chemistry textbooks, "Bixby? Bixby? Oh, you must be Katrina's mom. Theo's been telling me about you."

I groaned silently.

"Really?" said Mrs. Bixby, looking at me curiously.

I managed a weak smile. Normally, I would have felt embarrassed, but I was more worried about what was under the lid of the tray my mom was holding.

"You have another son, don't you?" Mrs. Bixby said. "I hear he's really bright."

"He's not here," Mom said shortly. Mom sure doesn't mind being rude when she feels like it. Mrs. Bixby didn't seem to like my mom much either, but she still had a big fake smile on her face. I had a feeling Mom wasn't going to be invited soon to any of Mrs. Bixby cosmetics parties.

Mr. Henley came up. He was carrying a

clipboard, which made him look more official and important than usual. "Time for the Bake-Off judging! What do we have here?" he asked Mrs. Bixby.

Mrs. Bixby turned her dazzling smile on him. "Strawberry Dream Cupcakes," she said and handed him one of the perfect cupcakes on a tiny pastel paper plate.

"Thanks!" said Mr. Henley.

As I watched him eat, I wondered if presentation was one of the things the judges would be scoring in the Bake-Off. If so, Mrs. Bixby clearly meant to ace the category. *Presentation* was way down on my list of worries. *Not being totally disgusting* was near the top. *Not causing people to throw up or get sick* was a close second, although I have to say my mom is a stickler about food safety.

"These are really good!" Mr. Henley said.

Of course.

"Okay, Theo," he said, looking down and making notes on his clipboard. "You're up next!"

Wait! Next? I tried to think of some clever reason to stall, maybe steer him away from our table, but there wasn't time. I had run out of lives. Game over.

"Now I haven't finished getting everything set up yet," my mom was saying, "but here." She held out the tray toward Mr. Henley and pulled off the lid.

CHAPTER 24

What is it? What are they? What did you make, Mom?" I leaned forward, trying to see around her.

"Oh yeah," Mr. Henley was saying, his mouth full of something that looked like a cupcake or muffin, probably containing sardines.

"What did you put in them?" I demanded,

reaching around Mom and grabbing one of the muffins from the tray.

"Theo!" Mom said. I knew I was being rude, but I was in a serious state of high anxiety.

I peeled back the cupcake liner and examined the golden yellow muffin closely. It smelled incredibly good.

"Spinach?" I asked suspiciously, remembering I had seen Mom with a bunch of it this morning.

"In lemon muffins? Honey!" Mom said, like I had suggested something completely bizarre. "No, the spinach is for dinner tonight."

That was a relief, but from the thoughtful expression on her face, I had a bad feeling that I might have given her an idea for a future food experiment.

The muffin in my hand was begging to be eaten, so I bit off a very tiny, tiny morsel. It was rich and buttery with a lovely, bright lemony taste.

"Did you use a starter lemon cake mix?" I asked.

"No."

"Lemon instant pudding?"

Mom just looked offended.

"Lemon extract?" I asked.

"No."

"Dextrose?"

"No, Honey!" my mom said. "I don't know where you get these ideas, Theo. Why don't you go with your friends, enjoy the FunFest? It looks like there's a ping pong ball race and a couple of other games for the kids."

"Uh, that's okay. I'd rather stay here with you and Grandma. How about Yellow 5 Lake? Did you put that in?"

"Certainly not." Mom turned her back on me.

I kept eating. The muffin was out-of-this-world amazing, and I couldn't figure out what the catch was. It was starting to really bug me. I ate another one.

My English teacher, Mrs. Hill, came up to Mrs. Bixby's table. She was holding a clipboard and a pencil too, so I knew she was one of the Bake-Off judges.

I hurriedly finished my second muffin and brushed the crumbs off my hands.

"Mmm. Strawberry!" Mrs. Hill said. She thanked Mrs. Bixby and drifted over to our table, making notes on her clipboard.

"Hey, Mrs. Hill." I was dying to see what she had written down on her clipboard, but I couldn't figure out how to get the right angle so it wouldn't look like that was what I was doing.

"Oh hello, Theo," she said. She smiled at my mom. "I'm Mrs. Hill, Theo's English teacher."

"Dr. Westly," Mom said, but in a friendly way. "Would you like to try one of our Sweet Lemon Muffins?"

"I would indeed! They look Wonderful! You know," she went on, "we'll be having Parent-Teacher conferences soon, but I wanted to tell you that Theo shows Real Talent. He may even be Gifted."

"Oh really?" Mom said, sounding unimpressed as she continued setting out muffins.

"Listen to Mrs. Hill, Mom," I said, nudging her. Toby is so extraordinarily brilliant that the rest of us are like tiny blips on the IQ chart.

"Oh yes," Mrs. Hill said. "SUCH an Active Imagination. And so VIVID. Well, it's been a pleasure, Dr. Westly. My, these muffins are Quite good!"

Both Mom and Grandma looked at me when

she left.

"I have no idea what she's talking about," I said. "Probably nothing. Forget about it. So. Polysorbate 60?"

"Theo!" said my mom. I could tell she was starting to get kind of annoyed with me. "It's just flour, butter, sugar, milk, and a few eggs."

My eyes narrowed. "No soy lecithin?"

"No. Okay, I put in about two teaspoons of a mixture of monocalcium phosphate, sodium bicarbonate, and cornstarch."

"That's just baking powder!" I said accusingly.

Mom shrugged. "You asked."

"Guar gum? Tetrasodium pyrophosphate??"

"No."

"What did you put in them?" I asked, my voice rising. Not knowing was driving me nuts! "What's making it taste like lemon??"

"Lemon," my mom said.

"You mean like from a real lemon?"

Mom frowned at me. "Are you sure you're quite all right, Theo? You've been acting very odd this afternoon."

Well, this changed everything.

All week I had been dreading what awful food Mom would bring to the FunFest, but these lemon muffins were fantastic! We actually had a shot at winning this Bake-Off contest. Katrina's mom may look all pretty and normal and perfect, but my mom is a food scientist and what she doesn't know about food isn't worth knowing. The Westly Family pride was at stake.

I tried to look very, very casual as I side-stepped over to Mrs. Bixby's table.

"Oh hi, Mrs. Bixby," I said, in what I hoped was my most ordinary tone of voice. "I'm a friend of Katrina's. Say, these look really good. What did you say they were?"

"Strawberry Dreams," she said. She handed me a plate like I was someone special. She has really, really blue eyes. I thought of those cuttlefish with eight arms that hypnotize little sand crabs before their sucker tentacles suddenly shoot out and pull them in.

"Um, thanks. They look really great." I took the pink cupcake quickly and retreated to our table.

I took a bite. Vanilla cupcake underneath. A bit dry. Even crumby. And that frosting was . . . whoa, SUPER sweet. Yikes.

Darnell and his dad wandered over to our table to say hello. I quickly finished Mrs. Bixby's cupcake and tried to pretend I hadn't been sampling enemy wares.

"How's it going?" I asked Darnell in an

undertone while Mom and Arlo were shaking hands.

"Yeah, okay. Everybody really likes Dad's éclairs."

I saw my mom pull Darnell's dad aside and say, "Can I talk to you about your restaurant for a minute, Arlo? I had this wonderful idea for shrimp burgers."

Shrimp burgers? Yuck!

There were lots of kids and grown-ups coming up to our table now, wanting muffins. Grandma had pulled out a stack of white paper plates and was setting out lemon muffins as fast as I could serve them.

Darnell kept looking around over his shoulder. "Have you seen Stew-Pot?"

"No, I'm sure he's fine," I lied.

Mrs. Delgado, my Spanish teacher was coming in our direction, parting the crowd like a cruise ship sailing through the ocean. She had a clipboard tucked under one arm. Another judge!

CHAPTER 25

*H*ola, Theo," Mrs. Delgado said, coming up to our table. *"¿Cómo estás?"*

"Hola, Senora Delgado," I replied.

"What do we have here?" she asked, her pencil hovering above the clipboard.

I thought I'd really get on her good side if I threw in a bit of Spanish from class, so I said, *"¿Me gustaría* to try our Sweet Lemon Muffins, Senora?"

"Te gustaría, Theo," Mrs. Delgado said, frowning. "Would *you* like to try, not Would *I.*"

That's what I get for letting Genius Baby do my Spanish homework.

Darnell covered his mouth with his hand to keep from laughing. I kicked him under the table.

"Hmm." Mrs. Delgado took a bite.

Katrina came back to her mom's table and then wandered over to stand next to Darnell.

"Oh hey, Theo," she said.

"Shh!" I was waiting for Mrs. Delgado to say what she thought of the lemon muffins.

"These are very good, Theo. Did you help make them?"

"No, my mom did everything," I admitted.

"They're really excellent. Is this your grandma here with you?"

"What? Oh, yeah. Mrs. Delgado, Grandma. Grandma, Mrs. Delgado."

Grandma just smiled without her teeth. It truly was a hideous hat.

Mrs. Delgado turned back to me. "Well, Theo, good luck in the Bake-Off! And I'll see you tomorrow in class. Don't forget there's a quiz on Monday."

Huh? What quiz? Why don't I ever remember about these things?

"Absolutely," I said. *"Adiós,* Senora!"

Katrina followed Mrs. Delgado to her mom's table. I was straining to hear them over the noise of the FunFest. Mrs. Delgado picked up a cupcake, but then she and Mrs. Bixby talked, a lot, until *finally* I saw Mrs. Delgado take a bite of the cupcake.

She chewed. I watched her swallow. Would she also think they were dry and a bit crumby?

Mrs. Delgado said, "They're very *pink,* aren't they?"

Someone in the crowd suddenly called out, "Hey, Baby!"

"Mom!" Darnell ran to his mom and folded himself around her.

"We had a long layover and I thought I'd stop by, Baby," Darnell's mom said, hugging him. She was still in her flight uniform.

Darnell's voice came out muffled. "I'm not a baby, Mom," but he kept hugging her.

"I know, Baby," she said. "Who's your friend?"

I waved and said, "Hey, Mrs. Samuels," like an idiot. But she wasn't interested in me, because she's known me for, like, forever.

"This is Katrina, Mom," Darnell was saying.

Mrs. Delgado was gone. I had missed the rest of whatever she had said to Mrs. Bixby.

"Hi," Katrina said to Darnell's mom, and they shook hands. Like grown-ups.

The band had stopped playing. My math teacher, Mr. Jennings, in his blue blazer and gold tie with the school mascot, was speaking into the microphone up on stage. "After today we are eighty percent towards our goal for the new gymnasium, so I think we can call the All-School FunFest a success. Great job! Thank you everyone for participating!"

Everybody cheered. Mom came back through the crowd and said, "Cynthia! I didn't know you were coming!" and she and Darnell's mom hugged.

"We're going to check out some of the games, Theo," Katrina said. "Want to come with us?"

"No, thanks. I think Mom needs me here." Mom and Cynthia were standing there, chatting away, which is great, but there were people lined up at our table.

Darnell and Katrina wandered off together and I heard Katrina say, "Your mom is really pretty!" and Darnell said, "Yeah, she's all right, I guess," but you could tell he was really proud.

I didn't have time to pay attention. We were really busy now. The muffins were flying. The stack of empty trays under our table kept piling up.

There was a stifled cry off to our right. Mrs. Bixby had run out! Grandma and I exchanged a secret high-five, but there wasn't time for celebrating. Our table was still going strong, thanks to Mom's monster-size industrial oven in our basement.

Mr. Jennings handed the microphone over to Mrs. Hill, who announced the winner of the silent auction and then introduced Mrs.

Delgado.

Mrs. Delgado pulled the microphone up. *"Buenos días, amigos y familias!"*

People clapped and everybody sort of settled down to listen to the results of the Bake-Off, so Grandma and I had a breather. Everybody except for my mom, of course, who was busy catching up with Cynthia like the two of them hadn't seen each other in a hundred years.

"How long are you going to be in town?" my mom was asking.

"Just 'til tonight. We're out on a red-eye to Honolulu."

"That sounds nice," my mom said.

I wanted to tell them to keep it down so we could hear Mrs. Delgado, but that would get me into trouble.

"The Stevenson Family, for their Snickerdoodle Swirl Cookies, in the Most

Creative category," Mrs. Delgado announced into the microphone.

"We should get together and have coffee next time you're in!" my mom said.

Yes, catch up then! I couldn't believe how casually Mom was taking this Bake-Off contest.

"The prize for Best Chocolate Dessert," Mrs. Delgado said, "goes to The Samuels Family Chocolate Éclair Bombs! *Felicitaciones!*"

We all clapped and Cynthia laughed and said to Mom, "That man can cook!"

I was happy for Darnell's dad and everything, but what I was REALLY waiting for was the final category announcement.

Grandma looked serene and calm. Mom was still yakking away. I glanced over at Mrs. Bixby. Even though she was our mortal enemy in Cakes, Cupcakes, and Muffins, for a moment

I felt a bond of sympathy with her. We were both white-knuckled, waiting for the results.

"And in the Cake and Muffin category," Mrs. Delgado said . . .

CHAPTER 26

The prize," Mrs. Delgado said, leaning toward the microphone, "goes to . . . ."

Out of the corner of my eye, I saw Mrs. Bixby stand straighter and tuck one loose hair behind her ear. Mom was talking to Cynthia, not paying attention at all.

"The Westly Family Sweet Lemon Muffins!" Mrs. Delgado announced.

I let out a whoop.

Cynthia hugged Mom. Then Mom hugged me, then Grandma, and over the clapping I heard my mom say, "It was the funniest thing, you know. I found this old recipe box in one of Mom's hatboxes up in the attic. I had forgotten about them. She and I used to make these muffins all the time when I was a kid. She had so many great recipes."

I looked over at Grandma, who was looking up at the ceiling and humming softly to herself, and I knew I was in the presence of a Jedi master. She caught me staring at her with my mouth hanging open and she winked at me.

I heard a smothered sort of noise from our left and looked over. I had forgotten all about Mrs. Bixby in the excitement. Mrs. Bixby was standing with her arms folded, holding her pink jacket together and trying to look happy, but I was pretty sure she was annoyed. You could tell she'd been really surprised. I even kind of felt a little sorry for her, now that we had won.

The school band started up again. People were starting to leave. Mrs. Bixby was folding up her plastic tablecloth. Mom and Cynthia finally woke up enough to help me and Grandma, although they were still talking the whole time we were clearing the table and getting the trays ready to go out to Mom's car.

I started putting the leftovers away and throwing out used paper plates and napkins. When I looked up, Mike Vickers was looming over the table, eating the end of a cinnamon-sugar donut. I was nervous at first, but there were lots of adults around, so I figured he couldn't hurt me too badly, and besides, he didn't look like he was angry.

"What did you bring?" he asked with interest, leaning over the table.

"Lemon muffins," I said. "We're packing up, but here, have one." I grabbed a muffin from the tray my mom was about to put away.

"Consider it an olive branch," I said. We had just won a prize and I was feeling pretty good.

"There are olives in here?" he asked suspiciously. I could see one fist curled under the table.

"No, Mikey. A peace offering."

Mikey shrugged. "You know I ain't got nothing against you yourself, Westly."

"I know," I said.

"Huh," Mikey said, licking his fingers. "Nice flavor. A little too chewy in the center? The top has a crunch that's good. Bet you could make a pretty awesome scone if you started with cold butter and added more flour."

My mouth was hanging open again.

"I'm just saying." Mikey wiped his hands on

his sweatshirt. "What's with you, Fish-face?"

I closed my mouth.

"I'll probably have to search you for lunch money, same as usual, just so you know."

"I know. See you tomorrow morning, Mikey."

"Okay. Tomorrow then."

"Yep."

He reached over and scuffed up my hair in the back. I *really* hate it when people mess with my hair.

"Who was that?" Mom asked, turning around. "Did you give your friend a muffin?"

"Yeah. I think he liked it."

"Oh good," said Mom.

CHAPTER 27

Darnell and Katrina both turned up again with spray-colored hair and animal face paint and holding hands.

"We killed in the Apple Relay," Katrina said happily. It's pretty surreal, talking to someone with whiskers on her face.

"Uh, yeah, that's great," I said.

"Hey, we heard your mom's muffins won! Isn't that cool?" she asked.

I was a little weirded out that she and Darnell were holding hands, but they both seemed okay with it.

"I think that's so amazing your mom is a scientist," Katrina went on. "I think I want to be a chemist when I grow up. Maybe I could talk to her sometime."

"Uh, sure. She is really creative. Just, uh." I was going to warn her that Mom's cooking usually isn't this good, but I decided to let it drop.

"Well, it looks like my mom is already packed up, so I should go. Bye, Darnell. See you tomorrow."

I eyed the color spray-job on his hair. "Dude, you look magically delicious. Has anyone ever told you green is *not* your color?"

Then I elbowed him in the ribs and told him to knock off the dopey grin.

When we got back home, I helped Mom unload the empty trays from the car and bring them into the kitchen. Grandma wandered away, taking long, scary-looking pins out of her hat.

The front door banged open and Toby came barreling in at top speed, followed by the grim Mrs. McKinney.

"Mrs. McKinney took you to Seven Seas Aquarium, and we saw the piranhas and the electric eels and we—"

Mrs. McKinney gave him a terrible look and Toby clamped his mouth shut.

"Oh hello!" my mom said, coming out into the hall, drying her hands on a kitchen towel. "How did it go? Thank you so much for taking him today!"

Toby was obviously bursting with excitement, but he didn't say anything for once.

"We had a passable afternoon," Mrs. McKinney said in her deep, stony voice. "Anthea told me the boy was bright, but he's not very good at following directions, is he?"

Mom opened her mouth to say something and then closed it.

"No need to see me out," Mrs. McKinney said, which was just as well because Mom and I were so surprised we stood frozen for a minute. All of us except Toby, of course, who was so excited that he was dancing up and down like he had to go pee until Mom let him run off to find Grandma so he could tell her all about his afternoon at the aquarium.

Around five o'clock I took a break from my homework and wandered downstairs. Genius Baby was sitting on Dad's lap while Dad read the September-October issue of *Sport Rocketry* to him. Personally, I'm not sure we should be encouraging this mania of Toby's about rockets.

When Toby wriggled down and trotted off to get a drink of water, I sat down on the sofa next to Dad.

"So Dad," I said, casually. "You didn't happen to hear anything about Seven Seas Aquarium today on the news, did you?"

"Uh, no."

"That's good," I said, getting up again.

"Hey, Theo," Dad began. "Didn't that rug in the hallway used to be upstairs?"

"Oh that," I said. "Grandma and I thought it looked better in the front hall."

Dad nodded. "I can see that," he agreed slowly. He gave me a funny look. "Why did you want to know about Seven Seas Aquarium?"

"It's nothing. We'll probably never know, so it can't have been too bad, right? Forget I asked," I said.

Dad shook his head. Like *I* was the crazy one in this family.

CHAPTER 28

Dinner that night was served with a bag of spiced air, to enhance, my mom said, the flavor of the turnip-spinach soufflé. Toby told me "enhance" is just a fancy way of saying "improve," and I happen to know nothing can improve the taste of turnips, or spinach. When I left next morning for school, the rotary evaporator was spinning downstairs in the lab, so we knew Mom was back to her usual mad scientist self.

"Okay, picture this," I said to Darnell as I joined him on the front steps and he handed me my breakfast burrito, "Jabba's Sail Barge against the Corsair AND the Black Pearl."

Darnell wasn't looking quite as into it today.

"Come on," I prodded him. "Two ships to one, but," I paused dramatically. "Deck cannons and R2-D2 *and* Princess Leia. Plus I'll bet Jabba could do some damage just by sitting on someone, or whacking them with his tail."

I demonstrated with a karate chop.

"Yeah, I guess. Maybe," Darnell said.

"What kind of sandwich do you have?" I asked.

"Italian cold cut. Are you going to mess with it again?"

"No," I said. "I think one bad experience will be enough. Toby explained it to me once. It's called 'aversion therapy.'"

"Man," said Darnell. I was waiting for him to tell me how brilliant I was, but he said, "What do you suppose Stew-Pot is going to do to us?"

"That's an interesting question," I said. "Let's find out."

I'll admit my heart was beating pretty fast. Frankly, I thought Darnell might turn and run at any moment as Stew-Pot's gang loomed closer and closer, but when he sidled over, Stew-Pot seemed like he was trying to act like he wasn't scared of *us!*

"Check his pockets, Mikey," Stew-Pot said.

"Really?" I complained to Mikey. "I thought we had made a breakthrough in our relationship."

"Shut up, Westly. Check his pockets, idiot."

"Yeah okay, Stew," Mikey said.

"Sasquatch called," I said while he was

turning my clothing inside out. "He wants his shoes back." I was starting to feel better and better each minute we were still alive and in one piece.

"He ain't got nothing, boss." Mikey reported.

I shrugged my jacket back on. "That's a double-negative, you cretin. And anyway 'ain't' isn't a real word."

Mikey cocked a fist at me. "What did you call me?"

"Settle down, tiger," I said. "I didn't mean it personally."

Stew-Pot has yet to think of checking my shoes. He's not exactly what you'd call a brainiac, and as for Mikey . . . well, there are many bright and promising career paths still open to him.

Stew-Pot gave Darnell a wary look. "What's in the sandwich, creep?" he asked.

"Wouldn't you like to know," I said.

He seemed to waver for a moment in indecision, and then he jerked his thumb at us. "Ahhh, get lost," he said.

Apparently I was still going to get shaken down daily for my lunch money, but if Darnell got to keep his lunch, I call it a victory. A small victory, but I'll take it.

"Yeah, that's right," I called after their retreating backs. "I know chemistry, and I'm not afraid to use it."

Darnell said, "Wow," in low, amazed voice.

"Enjoy your Italian cold cut," I said to Darnell. "And by the way, you're welcome."

We've just gotten so used to sharing that Darnell split my pizza with me at lunchtime anyway, but he also gave me half of his sandwich to eat.

There were folds of sliced ham and salami,

cheese, shredded iceberg lettuce, banana peppers, onions, and tomatoes sprinkled with Italian herbs, salt and pepper, red wine vinegar, and olive oil on a crusty sub roll. All this time I thought Stew-Pot was just saying it to be a jerk, but he was right. Darnell's dad is the best sandwich maker probably in the whole world.

Mr. Henley kept up a running commentary as he handed back the tests Friday afternoon in class. "Good job, Katrina. Darnell, good effort, maybe next time study a little harder. Stewart. Not so good. All those trips to the bathroom weren't helping you. And the next time you try to cheat, Mike Vickers, you might want to copy off the test of someone smarter."

Finally, he came to me. "Theo. Surprisingly good. And here I thought you weren't paying attention in class. Keep up the good work."

I flipped to the last page. Mr. Henley had

drawn a frowny face next to my extra credit answer, but he had written +1 next to it. I can live with that. I bet Katrina got all two points. I looked over my shoulder. She and Darnell were sitting next to each other looking so happy they almost looked smug, which is just annoying, but Darnell is a really good friend, so I'm happy for him.

Mr. Henley finished handing out the tests and walked back to the front of the room to start class.

As I was I turning around to see the board, I caught Stew-Pot's eye. He made an awful, mean face at me, but I noticed he did his best to avoid making eye contact after that.

CHAPTER 29

I pulled on my shirt and jeans and hurried down for breakfast Saturday morning so I'd have time to eat before meeting Darnell.

"Hey Mom," I called as I reached the bottom of the stairs. "Do we have a big cardboard box or something I can use?"

"How big?" my mom asked.

Dad and Toby and Grandma were sitting at the breakfast table in the kitchen. Toby had tied his wubbie around his neck so that it looked like a very ragged, fuzzy, blue superhero cape. Grandma had her teeth back in and was looking as sharp as ever. I'm pretty sure she leaves them out on purpose when she's pretending to be all helpless and innocent. She can fool everybody else, but I know the truth.

"Eggnog pecan waffles for breakfast," my mom said cheerfully, handing me a plate before I could say no. Actually, I don't mind these so much. The taste is a little strange, but you can substitute eggnog in a lot of recipes that use milk and eggs and kind of get away with it.

I slid into my seat and picked up my fork. "You know, a box big enough to fit the Pearl in. We're playing pirate ships."

Toby looked up alertly. "Can you play too?" he asked.

"No. No little kids," I said.

"Try the fried squash blossom," Mom said. "You might like it."

"Uh, later," I lied. I used the edge of my fork to nudge it off the waffle. Sure, it may be fried to a crispy golden brown on the outside, but you're eating something that belongs in a vase, not on a plate.

"I think I have a box large enough in the garage," Dad said thoughtfully.

"What are these orange chunks in the marmalade?" I asked.

"Carrots," Mom said. "You know how important it is to eat from the four food groups, and breakfast—"

"Is the most important meal of the day," I finished. "I remember. Do you think I could borrow the box for today?" I asked Dad.

"I can pull it out after breakfast."

"That'd be awesome, Dad." I slid my phone

out of my pants pocket and checked it. "Darnell's supposed to text me when to meet him."

"You could come too," Toby suggested hopefully. "Perhaps Darnell would like to help you construct a raw egg catapult. You also have a new experimental design for a hovercraft to test."

"Good for you," I said. I checked my phone again.

Einstein scratched at the door outside and Dad got up to let him in. Poor Einstein. I don't think he's used the dog door since Grandma and Toby's foam experiment. Right away he trotted over and took up his favorite spot under the table next to Toby's chair. Toby is still his favorite person in the world, even though I'm the one that gave him his own can of tuna fish yesterday.

Dad put his plate in the sink and said, "I'll go see about that box. I've got some things to do this morning, Tobster, but if Theo's busy with Darnell, maybe you and I could work on that *Mercury* space capsule model this afternoon. What about it?"

"Yes, please!" Toby agreed. He turned to me expectantly. "What am I doing with the pirate ships with Darnell?"

"We're having a fight," I said shortly. I had already revealed too much.

"You could help," Toby offered. "You have been interested for a long time in conducting experiments with incendiary range weapons."

"I'll bet you have," I said. "And the answer is still No."

Toby dropped his voice so only I could hear. "Did I know in his or her lifetime the average person generates enough saliva to fill a swimming pool?" he whispered.

"That's nice," I said, eating my waffle.

Toby put his head down on the table, trying to make me look at him. "There are human tumors called *teratoma* that can grow bits of hair and bone and actual teeth inside them."

"Uh-huh."

Toby gave up. He gave me his best offended, hurt look and slid off his chair. Einstein got up and padded after him.

I finally texted Darnell. *R u ready?*

There was a LONG wait.

Mom went into the pantry and started humming to herself. That left just me and Grandma.

I leaned across the table. "Okay, Grandma. I gotta know. Did you hide those old recipes, or were they in the hatbox to begin with?"

Grandma sniffed.

"Come on, Grandma!" I protested. "I KNOW you made it so Mom would find them."

"I don't know where you get such ideas, Theo," she said.

There was an awkward silence while Grandma picked at her oatmeal.

"Well, mostly I just wanted to say thanks." I finished lamely.

"I have no idea what you're talking about," Grandma said, "and you're welcome."

I *KNEW* it!

"Some people have to find their answers for themselves," Grandma observed. "You're a lot like your mother that way."

My phone dinged.

Cant 2day maybe 2morrow.

What?

"I gotta call Darnell," I said and got up and went out into the hall.

CHAPTER 30

Hey, D!" I said when he picked up. "What gives?"

"Uh," Darnell said. "I can't today. Katrina has cross-country practice in the morning, and then we're going to study Spanish at the library, and then we're going out for ice cream with her mom."

I took it like a man.

"Sure," I said. "Yeah, whatever. That's cool.

Um, have fun."

There was a pause.

"So, we're good, right?" Darnell said.

"Oh yeah, absolutely." I was crushed, but I probably would have done the same thing in his shoes. Nobody would be dumb enough to turn down a date with Katrina Bixby, even if it was to do something nerdy like studying together.

"See you tomorrow?" he asked.

"Definitely."

I went back into the kitchen and sat down at the table.

"Great," I said to no one in particular. "Darnell's totally blown me off to go hang out with Katrina and now I have nothing to do."

Mom's voice came from the pantry. "Didn't I hear Mrs. Delgado say you have a Spanish quiz on Monday?"

I groaned.

"Is Katrina that cute girl from the FunFest?" Grandma asked.

"Yeah."

"Good for him," Grandma remarked. "I told you she didn't like you that much, if you recall."

"Geez, Grandma! Anything else you want to say to make my day worse?"

"You could always play with Toby, dear," Grandma said. "He would like that very much."

"Seriously?? That's supposed to make me feel better?"

"He may be a genius," Grandma went on, "but in many ways he's a very ordinary little boy who wants to play with his big brother. Who knows, you might have a good time."

"I might as well play with him," I grumbled. "All my other friends have abandoned me."

"That's the spirit," Grandma said crisply. "I

think he's upstairs."

In the hall at the foot of the stairs, I turned back. "Hey, Grandma," I said.

She looked at me over the rim of her glasses.

"What kind of chemical reaction is it when one substance breaks down into two new substances?"

"Decomposition. You remember the elephant toothpaste we made?" she asked. "The H_2O_2 molecules break down into water, H_2O, and oxygen, O_2. What do they teach you in that science class of yours?"

"Thanks, Grandma. I was just curious." I grinned at her and went upstairs.

Einstein lifted his head to say hello.

"Hey, boy." I scratched him over his left ear in the way he likes and he thumped his tail.

The back end of Toby was sticking out of the linen closet. He had a plastic spray bottle and an old margarine tub, which must have come from the Nesbitts' recycling bin next door because Mom says she won't allow dangerous chemicals like hydrogenated soybean oil in the house.

"Uh, whatcha doing, Genius Baby?"

"Shhhh!" Toby said. "And don't turn on the overhead light. The worms won't like it."

"Do I *want* to know what weird science experiment you've got going on here?" I asked, getting down on my knees to look inside the dark closet.

"It's a worm garden," Toby said in a hushed voice. "Look, they've made tunnels in the dirt. Do I see?"

"Oh yeah, I see." And you could, which was actually kind of cool in a gross way. "Isn't that the aquarium that used to be in Dad's office?" I asked.

"He wasn't using it anymore," Toby said. He was peeling off the lid of the plastic tub. There were bits of brown banana and apple and grass clippings inside. "Breakfast time!"

I watched him drop food into the tank.

"Uh, what's that over there growing out of Dad's tennis shoe?" I nodded toward the mass of rubbery white tentacles curling and poking through the shoelace holes.

"A potato," Toby said, like it was the most obvious thing in the world.

"Does Dad know you borrowed his shoes?"

"It was required for a heliotrope experiment. He wasn't using them," Toby said. He was busy misting the worms with the spray bottle.

"He won't be using them now for sure. No wonder so many things go missing in this house. What else have you got up here?" I asked, poking my head farther into the closet.

"Nothing . . . here," Toby added, in a way that made me want to get up and go check my closet right away. He put his hand on the glass side of the aquarium. "You shall have to let them go soon," he said sadly to his little worm friends.

He is so WEIRD!

"The answer is 16, by the way."

"Huh?"

"How many friends Louise can invite to her party," Toby said patiently, like he was talking to someone very dumb.

"Oh," I said. "I already turned in my homework."

He shrugged. "You just thought I might like to know."

"Thanks."

Toby replaced the lid on the empty margarine tub and stood up, dusting his little hands together. Einstein heaved himself up onto his feet. Apparently we were done here.

My dad called up the stairs, "Theo! I've got that cardboard box for you from the garage."

I was about to tell him to forget about it when Toby's short, skinny arm shot out and stopped me.

"Yes, this is good," he said in an excited whisper. "We will need a box to make the mummified fish."

I stared at him.

"Sure, why not," I said. I leaned my head over the railing. "We'll take the box, Dad."

"And the fish in the refrigerator," Toby whispered.

Einstein pricked up his ears at the word *fish*.

"Uh, I'm pretty sure Mom was planning on using that for dinner tonight," I said.

"It's for science. She'll understand," Toby

assured me. "Besides, do I really want to know what Mom will make for dinner with a striped sea bass?"

That settled it. "You're right," I said. "I'll go get the fish."

"Also lots of baking soda and salt, to produce sufficient dehydration," Toby called after me.

"You mean like that astronaut ice cream stuff?" I asked, halfway down the stairs. "Just how big is this model of the *Mercury* spacecraft you're building with Dad?"

Toby rolled his eyes. "Not freeze-dried, mummified. But," he agreed, "the principle of removing water molecules to extend shelf-life and slow the rate of decay is similar."

"Sounds completely disgusting. Let's do it," I said.

EXPERIMENTS

IMPORTANT NOTE

Before you get started:

STEP 1: When performing these or any other science or cooking experiments, read the directions first all the way to the end so you know what's coming.

STEP 2: Make sure you have all the ingredients, materials, and equipment you will need before you get started so they're ready when you get to each new step.

STEP 3: Clear the area where you will be working. Decide where you will put things after you finish using them so they don't get in your way.

STEP 4: Lay out all your equipment.

STEP 5: Follow all warning and safety instructions, either in the experiment or on product labels.

STEP 6: Wash your hands, definitely before experimenting with food, and definitely after experimenting with chemicals.

LASTLY: A recipe is like a scientific hypothesis. Cooking is like doing an experiment to prove, or disprove, the hypothesis. If you get curious and want to start tweaking the recipes to create your own variations, keep a notebook to record what you tried and what you find out.

FOG MACHINE

Make sure you do this experiment in a well-ventilated area. This experiment is best done with a responsible adult, or a crazy grandma.

MATERIALS

3 Tablespoons distilled water (available in gallon jugs at most grocery stores)

1 Tablespoon glycerin (available online or at a pharmacy)

EQUIPMENT

Empty soda bottle (20-oz size)

Duct tape

Disposable aluminum pie pan

Large empty soup or coffee can

Large candle with three wicks

Funnel

Measuring spoons

Measuring cup

Spoon for stirring

DIRECTIONS

STEP 1: Combine distilled water and glycerin in the measuring cup and stir to make the fog juice. Set aside.

STEP 2: Assemble your fog machine by cutting off the top of an empty soda bottle so that it forms a dome. Set the bottle top in the middle of the pie pan. Bend the rim of the pie pan around the bottle and seal with duct tape so there are no leaks.

STEP 3: To construct a stand, ask an adult to help you poke ventilation holes in the bottom of large can.

STEP 4: Let 'er rip! Light the candle. Set the coffee can upside-down over the candle. Place the pie pan on top of the can. Use the funnel to pour about a teaspoon of fog juice through the neck of the soda bottle, then stand back.

SNOT-IN-A-BAG

There are lots of snot recipes online. Some of these include borax, a laundry detergent additive, as an ingredient. This is a dangerous chemical, so if you want to use borax, do it with a science teacher or other adult and make sure you follow all the warning labels.

Theo came up with another version here that uses gelatin and is safe for kids to do on their own. If you plan on keeping your bag of snot around for a couple of days, remember to store it in the fridge.

MATERIALS

1/4 cup cold water

1 drop blue food coloring

2-3 drops yellow food coloring

1 package gelatin

1/4 cup hot water

2 spoonfuls of white glue

3 spoonfuls of water

1/2 cup corn syrup

2 drops yellow food coloring

EQUIPMENT

Measuring cup

Spoon for stirring

Kitchen timer or stopwatch

Small bowl

Ziploc-style re-sealable bag

DIRECTIONS

STEP 1: Measure out 1/4 cup cold water. Add 1 drop of blue and 2-3 drops of yellow food coloring. Sprinkle the contents of 1 package of gelatin into the measuring cup and stir until the granules dissolve. Set a timer for 5 minutes.

STEP 2: Heat 1/4 cup water to boiling. When the timer goes off, pour the hot water into the cold water and stir to help the gelatin dissolve. Set aside.

STEP 3: In a small bowl, combine the 2 spoonfuls of glue and 3 spoonfuls of water. Add 1/2 cup corn syrup and 2 drops of yellow food coloring. Stir to combine.

STEP 4: Pour everything into a Ziploc-style bag. Check for leaks. Now SQUISH to mix.

STEP 5: Let your bag of "snot" rest in the refrigerator until it gels into something truly GROSS.

Note: Snot-in-a-Bag, especially the kind with borax, is not meant to be handled. If you do get some of it on you, wash your hands right away like Darnell does.

ELEPHANT TOOTHPASTE

You can find different versions of the Elephant Toothpaste experiment on the Internet that are safe to do at home. Grandma and Toby performed their experiment using potassium iodide as the catalyst, but you can test this out using yeast you can buy at a grocery store. Remember to set the bottle on a cookie sheet or large cake pan to catch the foam when it shoots out!

MATERIALS

1/2 cup hydrogen peroxide (3% solution)

Squirt of liquid dish soap

Squirt of food coloring (optional)

2-3 drops of peppermint oil or peppermint extract (optional)

1 packet dry yeast

3 Tablespoons very warm water

EQUIPMENT

Empty soda bottle (16 or 20-oz size)

Funnel

Measuring cup

Measuring spoons

Spoon for stirring

Cookie sheet or cake pan

Safety glasses

Rubber gloves

DIRECTIONS

STEP 1: Measure out the hydrogen peroxide and pour it carefully through the funnel into the plastic bottle. Add the liquid dish soap, food coloring, and peppermint, and give it a gentle swirl to mix. Set the bottle on a large cookie sheet. Preferably on a table. Preferably over a tile floor, not carpet.

STEP 2: Add the warm water to the small bowl or measuring cup. To activate the yeast the water should be warm enough to be almost hot, but not uncomfortably hot when you touch it. If you have a kitchen thermometer, test the water temperature. Ideally it should be between 110 and 115 degrees. Pour in the packet of dry yeast and stir to dissolve the yeast.

STEP 3: Now the safety glasses. Rubber gloves are also a good idea. Using the funnel, carefully pour the dissolved yeast into the plastic bottle and stand back!

DRINKABLE BLOOD

The wikiHow website www.wikihow.com includes many recipes for fake blood you can experiment with making, some of which are drinkable. Grandma and Toby tweaked this simple drinkable blood recipe by substituting milk instead of water. Food coloring can stain, so don't drink it on the couch!

INGREDIENTS

1 cup milk

1 cup light corn syrup

1/2 cup chocolate syrup

5-6 drops red food coloring

EQUIPMENT

Small mixing bowl

Measuring cup

Spoon for stirring

DIRECTIONS

STEP 1: Pour the milk into a glass or mixing bowl. Add the corn syrup and chocolate syrup and stir well.

STEP 2: Add the chocolate syrup and the red food coloring. Keep stirring, tasting, and adding more food coloring or chocolate syrup until you have the consistency, color, and taste you want.

This recipe makes two servings, so you can share it with a friend.

GRANDMA'S SWEET LEMON MUFFINS

There are lots of great recipes and variations for traditional lemon poppy seed muffins in cookbooks and online to experiment with baking. This is a simplified sweet lemon muffin to get you started.

Many recipes use lemon cake mix or lemon instant pudding as an ingredient. All of the food additives Theo asks his mom about are real sub-ingredients that can be found in these types of recipes. The recipe Dr. Westly found in Grandma's old hatbox uses fresh ingredients.

INGREDIENTS

1 stick (1/2 cup) butter, melted

1/4 cup milk

1/2 cup lemon juice (bottled, about 3 lemons)

1 cup sugar

2 eggs

1 1/2 cups flour

2 teaspoons baking powder

EQUIPMENT

Kitchen timer or stopwatch

Baking spray

One 12-cup or two 6-cup muffin pans

Measuring cup

Medium-size mixing bowl

Rubber spatula or large spoon for stirring

Measuring spoons

Fork for stirring

Toothpick or 1 strand uncooked spaghetti

Hot mitt or potholder

Wire rack

Plastic knife

DIRECTIONS

STEP 1: The first step involves a little kitchen chemistry. Pour the milk into the measuring cup, add the lemon juice, and set a timer for 10 minutes. The acid of the lemon juice reacts with the protein (casein) in milk. Normally the molecules of casein have a negative charge, but when the pH of the milk is lowered by adding an acid, the negative charge is neutralized and the casein starts to clump together, producing curdled milk (curdling is good in this recipe).

STEP 2: Preheat the oven to 350 degrees so that it will be hot when your muffins are ready to be baked.

STEP 3: Grease the muffin pan(s) using baking spray or extra butter and set aside, so they'll be ready when you need them.

STEP 4: Combine your dry ingredients: Measure out the flour. Measure the baking powder and add to the flour in the measuring cup, stirring with a fork to combine. Set aside.

STEP 5: Combine your wet ingredients: Melt the butter (you can do this quickly by microwaving it for about 45 seconds on 50% Power). Pour the melted butter and sugar into a mixing bowl and stir with a rubber spatula. Add the egg and stir again. When the timer goes off, add the curdled milk and stir once more.

STEP 6: Now add the dry ingredients into the wet ingredients. The sodium bicarbonate in the baking powder starts reacting with the citric acid in the lemon juice right away, so you want to stir just enough to make sure the ingredients are combined and then quickly spoon the batter into the muffin pan(s).

STEP 7: Bake the muffins at 350 degrees for 20-25 minutes. Pull the pan out of the oven at 20 minutes to test for doneness by poking a toothpick or uncooked strand of spaghetti in the center of a muffin. If it comes out clean, the muffins are done. If the center of the muffin is still soft and sticky, put the muffins back in for another 5 minutes and then test again. After the muffins are done, use a hot mitt to pull the pan out of the oven and set it on a wire rack. Let the muffins cool for 10 minutes and then use a plastic knife to gently loosen them so the muffins come out of the pan. Allow the muffins to finish cooling on the wire rack.

Makes 12 muffins

Note: Dr. Westly is considering putting spinach in her next batch of muffins to add iron and other important vitamins like A, C, E, K, and the B vitamins Thiamine, Niacin, B6, Folate, as well as important trace metals such as manganese, magnesium, potassium, calcium, phosphorus, potassium, and zinc, but she's not sure how adding spinach will affect the taste . . . .

ARLO'S CHOCOLATE ÉCLAIR BOMBS WITH REAL DEAL PASTRY CREAM

This recipe comes in two steps: 1) experimenting with pastry cream, and then 2) assembling the éclair bombs. If you want to, you can skip the pastry cream and use store-bought vanilla pudding to make the éclair bombs.

Making pastry cream is molecular chemistry for the kitchen. Proteins in the egg yolk which are liquid at room temperature start to break apart (denature) and then clump together when heated. But if they get too hot (imagine cracking an egg into a hot skillet), the egg cooks into a solid. To get pastry cream, or any other type of custard, the eggs have to be heated just enough, very slowly, to start to thicken.

It takes practice to make pastry cream because you have to get the timing right on each of the steps. There are also parts when it feels like you need three hands, so you might want to get someone to help the first couple times.

By itself, the Real Deal Pastry Cream recipe makes 1/2 cup, about 2 servings. When you get the pastry cream right, you can triple the recipe to make enough for 6 Chocolate Éclair Bombs.

INGREDIENTS

REAL DEAL PASTRY CREAM

To Practice

1/2 cup milk (whole or 2%)

2 Tablespoons sugar

1 Tablespoon cornstarch

1 egg yolk

For 6 Éclairs

1 1/2 cups milk

6 Tablespoons sugar

3 Tablespoons cornstarch

3 egg yolks

ASSEMBLING THE ÉCLAIRS

1 package (6-count) frozen pastry shells

Chocolate syrup for drizzling

EQUIPMENT

Measuring cup

Small pot or saucepan

Measuring spoons

3 small bowls

Small bowl (something heatproof that won't melt)

Whisk

Rubber spatula or large spoon

Bowl for the finished pastry cream

Plastic wrap

Baking sheet

Hot mitt or potholder

Wire rack

DIRECTIONS

STEP 1: Timing is critical to getting this recipe to work, so lay out your equipment and ingredients before you start. Pour the milk into the pot and set it on the counter. Measure out the sugar and cornstarch into two of the small prep bowls. Now you're ready to master separating the egg.

STEP 2: Set the remaining small prep bowl next to the mixing bowl. Crack the egg as cleanly as you can, once or twice around the middle, so the shell forms two halves. When the eggshell comes apart, quickly catch the yolk (it's slippery!) in one half, and let the egg white slide into the prep bowl. Pour the yolk back and forth between the eggshells, letting as much of the egg white spill out as you can, but being careful not to break the yolk. Plop the egg yolk into the mixing bowl. This recipe doesn't use the leftover egg whites, but they can be made into an egg white omelet, or used in another recipe.

If you're having trouble separating eggs, there are inexpensive kitchen gizmos available for straining whites or plucking out yolks.

STEP 3: Now that you've got the egg yolk in the mixing bowl, it's time to put the pot with the milk in it on the stove and turn on the heat to the lowest setting. You're about to do two things at once, so you want to pay attention.

STEP 4: WHILE the milk is simmering, add the sugar to the mixing bowl with the egg yolk and whisk it together into a thick yellow paste. Next, add the cornstarch and whisk it again until there's no white left. It will be very thick. Keep checking your milk to make sure it isn't starting to boil.

STEP 5: When you start seeing bubbles in the milk, take the pot off the stove and over to your mixing bowl (you're leaving the stove on, so be careful). Here's where it would be useful to have three hands. You want to very slowly drizzle the hot milk into the bowl WHILE whisking quickly, so the egg doesn't have a chance to fully cook (curdling is bad in this recipe). Keep whisking, pausing with the milk if you need to, to make sure there are no clumps.

STEP 6: Keep whisking! When all the milk is in the bowl, bring the empty pot BACK to the stove and then pour the mixture in the bowl back into the same pot. Put the bowl to one side and concentrate on whisking the liquid in the pot. Everything is going to happen in the next 1-2 minutes.

STEP 7: As you whisk, you'll see the liquid start to change. It will start to look fluffy with lots of bubbles, and then all of a sudden, it will start to thicken up. Right away, you want to take the pot off the stove with one hand, while whisking like crazy with the other so that the pastry cream stays smooth as it finishes thickening (you're leaving the stove on again until you have a hand free to turn it off, so be careful). It will look a lot like vanilla pudding at this point.

STEP 8: Put your whisk aside and quickly use a rubber spatula or spoon to scrape the pastry cream into a bowl you can put in the refrigerator. Put the pot down somewhere safe (it's still hot). Turn off the stove. Cover the warm pastry cream in the bowl with a piece of plastic wrap and press down gently. The plastic wrap keeps the surface of the pastry cream from getting rubbery as it cools. Put the bowl into the refrigerator and let the pastry cream chill for 4 hours.

TO ASSEMBLE THE CHOCOLATE ÉCLAIR BOMBS

STEP 9: A true éclair is made with *pâte à choux* pastry, which Arlo makes from scratch, but you can use frozen puff pastry dessert shells to save time. Follow the directions on the package to bake the pastry shells on a baking sheet. Cool about 10 minutes on a wire rack.

STEP 10: Spoon the chilled pastry cream into the baked shells and drizzle with chocolate syrup.

ABOUT THE AUTHOR

H.J. HEWETT is a compulsively experimental cook who happens to be related to several super-smart (and slightly crazy) people she loves who like to tinker with science. This is her first book for kids.

CRAZY GRANDMA, GENIUS BABY & ME

Cover design by Robert E. Hewett

ISBN: 1979790809
ISBN-13: 978-1979790802

FOR ROSEMARY & ARI, THE ORIGINAL CRAZY GRANDMA AND GENIUS BABY

ACKNOWLEDGEMENTS

I am grateful for the feedback and advice of: Emily Bereiter, Michael Beranek, Jessica Campbell, Nicole Fruit, Ilene Goldman, Jean and Joan Hewett, Logan Jacot, Beth Klein, Christine Lee, Gary Lumpp, Susan and Kay Manolis, and Jack Walrath, and for the love and support of my parents, Bob and Rosemary, and my husband, Bob.